Wishing He Was My Savage

Trenae

Wishing He Was My Savage

Copyright © 2017 by Trenae

Published by Mz. Lady P Presents

Dedication:

This book is dedicated to my cousin, Christiana Finesse.
Without you this book wouldn't have been completed. You
are always there when I need you, no matter the favor you
always come through. Words can't express how grateful I am
for you. Thank you, a million times!

Ava Marie. Anything I do is for my light bright god-child.
Nanny loves you and will move heaven and earth to make you
smile.

To my sister, Asia Lewis. We the girls of the crew and swear
we stay live! I can't thank you enough for giving me the
opportunity to know and love Ava! Love ya gah.

To my brother, Kevin Lewis Jr. My giant I'm so proud of you
for following your dreams and never giving up. You went to
college and dominated the court as well as those classes and
graduation is coming up. Love you my big lil brother.

A Very Special Dedication:
I dedicate this entire series to Ashley Nicole Metz. Ashley is the beauty that graces the covers of the series and I am honored to have the permission to use her photo. Though she was taken from this earth at a very early age, Ashley touched so many people in Lafayette, Louisiana and surrounding areas. When you mentioned greatness that came from the area, you had to mention our favorite model. For any photographer and model that worked with the beauty, you knew being in her presence was a blessing. Ashley, you are missed and will never be forgotten. Fly High Black Butterfly.
To Mrs. Carla and Ziggy, there is beauty in your strength! Thanks for sharing Ashley with us all.

Acknowledgments

Seventh book Shawttttyyy!!!! Lol

This part never gets easy because of course I don't want to miss anyone. First and foremost, I want to thank God for giving me the gift of storytelling. I'm still shocked that I can actually create a story that you, my readers, love. It baffles me that I went through so much schooling just to end up coming back to what I've always loved, writing. I know it was only God's doing. Without him there would be no Trenae' and for that I am forever grateful.

To my parents, Trudy, Keith and Tarunye, thank you for the continued support. As soon as I say my book is live and you all will quickly one-click and I definitely appreciate it.

To the women who played a huge role in raising me, my grandmother Deloris, my aunt Betty, and my aunt Mona, I appreciate every sacrifice you made to make sure I never went without anything I needed. Thank you for all that ya'll do.

To my siblings, Kevin, Malika, Asia, Tarya, Makia, and Jayanma I love ya'll and never forget that the sky is the limit.

To my Godchild and constant headache, Ava, anything that I do is for you! It's my job to make sure that smile never falls from your face and I'll work overtime to make sure that happens. Nanny loves you forever and a day Phat-Phat!

To my cousins that are more like siblings, Terrance (Keep ya head up cuz), Raquel, Reggie, Trevor and Boots I love ya'll!

To my squuuuuaaaadddd lol, Chrissy, Fantasia and Kelleashia bruh so many of ya'll stories find their way into my books. My characters are based off ya'll and everything, thanks for the constant laughs. Above all that thanks for remaining the same, ya'll never switched up on the kid and I appreciate that. You know ya'll stuck with me foreva (Cardi B voice).

Keondria, Secret, Kelleashia, Zatasha and Rikida, I can't thank ya'll enough for the brutal honesty ya'll give me. Ya'll been rocking with me since The Sins of Beretta one and as I end their story here you are all, still by my side. Ya'll the best.

To my sisters in pen, AJ Davidson, Latoya Nicole and Manda P. Ya'll motivate me like no other and I love ya'll for that. We will keep dropping banger after banger until our idols become our rivals.

To my publisher, the creator of my baby King, the literary grim reaper and the banger dropper herself, Mz Lady P!!! I can't thank you enough honey. You took a chance on me and I appreciate that forever. As I'm learning you as a publisher and a friend your hustle rubs off on me. You push me more than I have ever been pushed in my life. You inspire me more than you know!

To my sisters of KBC thanks for ya'll continued support, Love ya'll.

Last but most certainly not least, to YOU my readers, I cannot thank you all enough for continuing to rock with me. Ya'll took a chance on a new author and I will strive to never let ya'll down. Thanks for the inboxes and reviews on my past work, I definitely took everything ya'll said into consideration. I have to also thank ya'll for being patient with me, as I got this book done for you all.

If I missed anyone know that it wasn't intentional. Charge my memory and not my heart for that mistake.

I hope you enjoy my new series because these characters took me for a ride and never stopped talking to me!

Want to keep up with Trenae'?

Facebook: Paree Trenae

Facebook: Author Trenae'

Instagram: Trenaedhaplug

Twitter: Ooh_Paree_Dear

Snapchat: PareeTrenae

Periscope: PareeTrenae

Add my reader's group: Trenae' Presents: The Juice

Table of Contents

Chapter 1

Ashleigh

"Ayyyyeeee my best bitch has graduated!" Without turning around, I was positive that my super ghetto best friend Amanda was the owner of that outburst. I wanted to fuss about that but I could only smile when I spun around and saw at least two dozen roses and tons of balloons in her hands.

"For me, oh my gosh you shouldn't have!" I said in the most proper voice I could muster. "Girl you look bomb!" I complimented her clothing. If Amanda did nothing else, her ass could dress.

"Oh, you mean this old thing!" She spun around in the strapless, wide leg jumpsuit she was rocking the hell out of. "You know all I do is dress, impress then rest." She laughed as I hugged her. I couldn't help but to sneak a look around the entry way to the Cajun Dome and drop my head in disappointment.

"Congrats Ash!" I heard a fellow classmate say and I smiled and wished them the same. It was a long road but I finally had my business degree in hand and was well on my way to opening my very own business. I had dreams of becoming the owner of a small but successful beauty salon and I also wanted to branch out and dabble in the virgin extension business. You can't go wrong when you mix the two. Looking at the huge smile on Amanda's face did nothing but make me feel bad. I wanted to turn up and celebrate with my girl but the pain I felt in my heart wouldn't allow me to. Pulling out my cellphone I quickly looked over the countless "congrats" and "sorry I can't make its" before I found the contact that I was looking for and sending a text.

Dre: I don't know why I always expect you to be a different man then what you have been over the years. I always want to see the good in you but I don't think there is any. I thought for once I would come before that damn bottle, I guess not. Thanks for ruining the most important day of my life asshole!

After hitting send I bit at the inside of my cheeks so I wouldn't allow the tears I felt to fall. This couldn't be Dre and I had been in this tragedy of a relationship for about three years. Him not being at one of the most important events of my life thus far doesn't surprise me at all but that doesn't make it hurt any less. When we first started dating it wasn't a fairytale but it was close as shit. I made some money braiding hair and Dre had an amazing job at a plant in Baton Rouge. We lived comfortably and were in the honeymoon aspect of our relationship. You know the point where everything was going good. He could do no wrong in your eyes and you could do no wrong in his. Ya'll I loved Dre's dirty drawls. I swear the elders know what they are talking about. I heard once before, every old broom sweeps good, and never understood it until everything came crashing down. When we were good we were perfect.

Then came the drinking. At first, I noticed he would have a glass or two of hard liquor after work, to wound down as he called it. He really had no preference, one day he would be drinking Hennessy and the next he would be drinking patron. Liquor was liquor to him. I was fine with that until it became a bottle or two. Anytime I pointed out the fact that he was consuming too much liquor I was an ignorant hoe or an annoying bitch. After he sobered up he apologized and would buy me some fancy bag or shoes I didn't need or want and I would forgive it all. Our fairytale came to a tragic end when Dre decided getting drunk after work wasn't enough. He took the forty-five-minute drive to Baton Rouge, Louisiana after downing a couple of glasses of Henny. Thank God, he didn't hurt anyone on the way their but I can't say the same about once he got there. I was told he was fucking up orders the whole day and picking arguments. One of the men he started an argument with, reported the smell of alcohol to his boss and since they were cool his boss warned him and told him go home for the day. Instead of leaving like a smart man would, he confronted the worker and ended up getting into a full-blown fight that resulted in him getting fired and arrested. Somehow, I was to blame for that incident.

"Earth to my bestie!" Amanda snapped her fingers in my face. "If you cry over pussy ass Dre I will kick your ass first then go bust the windows out of his car." Amanda said and I knew that this wasn't a threat it was a promise that she would see through. I was far from a push over but out of the two of us, Amanda was always the one that got shit popping. If we ever ended up in jail together, I swear it was her fault. Our attitudes were night and day but I loved her more than I could put into words. She was my best bitch!

"I just don't understand. Why couldn't he get himself together just this once? It's almost like he is jealous about my success. What did I ever do to him for him to constantly shit on me like this? Can't he see that I'm the only motherfucker in his corner? His family doesn't even fuck with his drunk ass anymore and he still gives me his ass to kiss." I said as a tear escaped.

"Oh, baby fuck no." Amanda said grabbing my arm and leading me away from the crowd of happy families and graduates that were taking pictures. "You will not cry over him on today. Tomorrow, I will allow you to cry on my shoulder and then go cook his meal." When I snatched my arm from her and shot her a look that would kill she simply rolled her eyes and kept walking, leaving me to follow as she spoke. "You know I'm not lying so you can save that lil attitude you just tried to cop. You get mad at everyone but the source of your unhappiness and that ain't cool. Now like I was saying, I'm here for you and you know that. I normally sit down and bring the snacks to your pity party but not today. He can have tomorrow but he will not cloud your mind on your big day. You worked too damn hard to give yourself a headache and just head home afterwards. No matter what he does you aren't leaving him. I'm not one to judge because I know more than anyone, the heart wants what the heart wants. You'll leave when you have enough. Until then let's go celebrate your day." She said hitting the locks to her Benz as I melted into the soft seats.

"Please hit that air?" I said as soon as she pushed the start button. The summer in Louisiana was a different type of hot. There was no breeze and at times I felt like we personally did the sun something. It felt like that bitch was beefing with us and wasn't letting up. The temperature was supposed to be in the 80s but I'm sure we were tap dancing on the 100s, because it was so hot.

"Yeah let me blast that motherfucker because bitch I can see your edges curling and your mug melting from over here." She cracked jokes at my expense. I know she was just trying to get a smile out of me and that's just what she got as we sat at my favorite table in Cheddar's downing drinks. She wanted to hit the road and take me some place nice but I wasn't in the mood for a road trip and besides, I genuinely loved Cheddar's. Their food was bomb and the painkiller drink they offered really was life.

"You know what, you were right. It is my fucking day!" I stated feeling the effects of that first drink take over me. "Fuck Dre, and all the liquor bottles I know are laying around on my living room floor." I declared.

"Yaaaassssss!" Amanda agreed.

"I am a college graduate!" I snapped my fingers.

"Say that shit!" she egged me on.

"I ain't some no future having bitch! I am about to be the boss of some shit!" I kept going feeling myself.

"You better flaunt that shit!" Amanda laughed.

"You know what I'm going do. I'm going get Dre back for all the times I had tears on my pillow." I smiled.

"Yaaaaasssss!" she still entertained me.

"I'm going cheat!" I nodded my head like it was a genius idea.

"Oh, bitch sit down." She rolled her eyes and began eating her food like what I said was bullshit.

"What?" I was confused on her attitude change."

"Look, your ass ain't going cheat so don't lie to the both of us. I want nothing more than you to cheat. I want nothing more than for you to run into a nigga with a dick so big he rearranges some organs. I want that nigga to fuck you so deep his dick knocks Dre simple ass right out of your bed. But bitch in order to do that your ass has to stop acting like Dre has eyes on you at all times." She said biting her shrimp and discarding the tail on the side of her plate.

"Buttttt Manda, I'm so serious." I whined. "I'm going cheat and I'm going make babies on his ass. Then because I love him so much, I'm going come back and make him raise another nigga babies." I said.

"Bitch you really are tripping." She laughed at my plan.

"You just watch, I'm going throw this pussy at a boss." I laughed just as a man walked over to us.

"Excuse me, I was watching the game with my friends and you caught my eyes. I see you graduated today." He observed nodding towards the cap that sat on my head. He was so fine words wouldn't come out. The 360 waves he rocked and his beard had me licking my lips. Speaking of lips, his were so damn sexy I almost came on myself when he pulled the bottom one in between her teeth.

"Yeah my girl did!" Amanda answered for me.

"Beauty and brains, I like that. My name is Hezikye but my friends call me Kye." He introduced himself while sticking his hand out for me to shake. When I placed mine in his he placed a soft kiss on it.

"I'm taken!" I blurted out before I could stop myself. The chuckle he let out and the fact that Amanda suddenly asked for the check let me know I had fucked up. Who was I kidding? I was in love with an alcoholic and I wouldn't cheat if someone paid me to. Saying our goodbyes to Kye made my gloomy mood bounce back like it had never left. Amanda was silent the whole way to my house and only said something once we parked in my driveway.

"I love you Ash. You are an amazing woman and I can't wait until you see that you deserve better then he can offer you." She said pulling me into a hug. Stepping out of the car I ducked down until my eyes met hers again.

"The thing is I know, I just don't know what to do with that information." I confessed before shutting the door and walking up the walkway. Before entering my key and opening the door I said a quick prayer that I could have a peaceful night with my kindle. It was only five in the evening and I was already trying to end this day.

Stepping in my home my eyes involuntarily rolled. My job at AT&T'S call center allowed me to have a comfortable two-bedroom home and a used Altima that I loved. Because I paid for these things alone, I took pride in that. Dre never got the memo. He was sprawled out on my couch like affordable home furniture pulled half from his account for it monthly. Beer as well as Cîroc bottles littered the floor and was accompanied with McDonald's wrappers. Bypassing the mess, I stomped to the back of the house where my room was. That's right, we slept in different rooms. All it took was for me to roll over in his vomit one day for me to decide on that move. Whenever either one of us was feeling freaky we would venture into the other's room, fuck then dip. I quickly slipped out of my heels and clothes and into a nightgown and house slippers.

"I'm so sick of this shit." I mumbled to myself as I walked to the kitchen, grabbed the trash bags and loudly threw bottles into the trashcan. After I got to the last bottle I save the trash can and was startled by Dre leaning on the island in the kitchen.

"You had to make all that fucking noise? You shouldn't have left the house with it dirty any fucking way." He spat.

"It was my graduation day, Dre! And my house was spotless when I left this morning anyway!" I spat back.

"You been getting loose at the lip lately. I'm telling you right now to take your ass in that room and go to sleep." He said like I was his fucking child. I didn't feel like arguing and wanted to be alone anyway so I walked past him with plans of reading a book by AJ Davidson called, Cherished by a Boss. I heard him mumbling and ignored his ass. "Talking about some, my house. Like this only belongs to her." I heard which cause my blood to boil. Spinning around I could no longer bite my tongue.

"Yes, my home! That's in my name! Which I pay the bills for with my money! I'm so fucking sick of this Deandre! I AM NOT YOUR SLAVE!" I screamed at his back.

"Shut the fuck up." He calmly replied.

"I will not! I am so stupid for sitting here and dealing with this. You know how many men would be happy to have me in their..." before I could finish Dre made his way to me. In seconds, he grabbed my face with the palm of his hand and slammed the back of my head into the wall repetitively until I passed out. This couldn't be love.

9

Chapter 2

Amanda

Pulling into my garage I couldn't help the sadness that overcame me. Outside looking in, people would say I had it made. I was living the life that chicks my age didn't even have the imagination to dream up. I had just pulled my brand spanking new Benz into the garage of my very own four bedroom, three-bathroom home. My mini palace was designed by one of the best interior designers in Louisiana and it looked like a page straight from Home & Garden. Right beside my Benz was my custom painted matte black Audi that I only pulled out when I was stunting on someone. I didn't have to answer to anyone because I didn't work for anyone. I shopped when I wanted to, I hopped on a flight and woke up in different area codes when I wanted to and I didn't have no nigga nagging me. See even ya'll are fooled by the appearance and think I have it made. Trust me it's only because you are on the outside looking in. The house, the cars, the trips, the money. I swear I would give all that shit up if I could rewind time. None of this shit excites me because I paid the ultimate price for it all.

Unlocking the door, I walked into the kitchen where I was greeted with the soothing sounds of Toni Braxton. I hated coming back to a quiet or a dark house so I always left the kitchen light on and my sound system on. Kicking my heels off at the door I quickly disabled my alarm before the annoying buzzing began. Scooping my heels into my arms I treaded to the refrigerator where I damn near drooled at the thought of the bottle of wine I had waiting for me.

"Cause you came along and changed my life. Told me things would be all right!
And they were thanks to you. And now I have the strength to carry on, in my heart you have a home. And I never want to be alone! I love me some him, I'll never love this way again!" I sang along with Toni as I grabbed the bottle of wine then made my way to the living room. "You always said, good thing I was pretty because I couldn't sing for shit Mannie. I'm starting to believe you were right." I laughed to keep from crying as I spoke to the huge picture of him. This was the part of Amanda no one saw. When I was in public I was the life of every party. Oh, but when I came home I fell to pieces. My heart cried every night and I don't think that would change. I poured a glass of wine and downed it as I stared at the image. It was a picture of happier days. It meant the world to me because I was the photographer that captured the image. I remember when I first took it and couldn't help the smile that placed itself on my face. The memory made me so happy it hurt that I would never that way again.

"Aye Panda, bring yo ass here girl." Hearing him call out for me by the nickname he gave, I quickly abandoned my cell phone on the bed and met him in the living room.

"Why you screaming babe? What's wrong with you?" I asked.

"A nigga missed yo ass shawty. I needed to place my eyes on yo fine ass so this weak feeling would go away." He said placing his hands on my ample ass and pulling me close. The kiss he placed on my lips was rough but I felt the love in it. There wasn't a soft bone in Mannie's body and I learned to love that. I used to think I would want a soft ass man that catered to me, but that proved to be false. I needed a thug in my life because there was no way a momma's boy could handle me.

"You just left an hour ago Mannie." I giggled. "You said you had something important to do, are you finished already?" I asked.

"Shit there is only one thing more important to me than spending the day with you ma." He replied in his raspy voice with a smirk.

"And that is?" I asked. If it was business he would have told me because we had no secrets. I knew all of what he dabbled in.

"Last night remember you asked me to take your picture before the club? Yo ass let me have it for not centering you in the pic. Then you told me you knew all that fancy shit cause you wanted to be a photographer before your parents died." My mouth dropped because I was just rambling and didn't think he was paying me any attention. When he motioned behind me there were tons of best buy bags. Running to them I cried tears of joy when I saw all the items he had. "Ma, your parents died, as tragic as that is that doesn't mean your goals and dreams left with them. As long as there is a breath in my body and blood in my veins you better chase your dreams." I ran to his arms and collapsed in them.

"Mannie, I love you more than I can put in words. I have no idea what I would do without you and I never want to find out." I cried. "I can't believe you did this for me."

"Ma listen, if shit ever go left with us or for some reason I ain't here with you and you have to move on. Get you a nigga that will move heaven and earth just to see you smile. It's no such thing as you want something and I can't provide it. I will rob my fucking aunt Ray, and she my momma favorite sister, to make sure you never go without." He told me staring me in my eyes. "Nah hook that shit up, I'm going change." He said walking away.

"Where are we going?" I asked him sadly. I didn't want to leave, I wanted to play with my new equipment.

"Shit I'm going put on a suit or something. I'm going get my Tyrese on and model for yo ass." He called over his shoulder making me fall out laughing.

I laughed looking at him in the suit and fresh pair of Jordan's. Mannie was my first and most likely the only love I would ever have. The cause and cure of my pain is Emmanuel James Powers. Mannie made me the woman I am today, literally. When I ran into Mannie, I was a lost and confused 16-year-old teenager that had just lost her parents. The streets that my parents loved dearly, are the reason they are six feet under now.

After their death, I was doing whatever to ensure that child protective services didn't catch up to me. I knew all about the homes that children ended up in and refused to be some perverts favorite play toy. With only months until my seventeenth birthday I was confident that I could find a job and at least rent a room for someone until I figured out what my next move would be. I remembered the day I ran into him like yesterday.

"Umm can I just have a double cheese burger and a cup for water?" I asked the woman behind the counter of McDonald's. I watched as her eyes traveled up the length of my body and her nose frown up as she judged me. I crossed my arms over my chest hoping she wouldn't see the many stains on my shirt. I had just taken the change I had and washed my clothing at the laundry mat up the street so this was all I had until my clothes dried.

"Make sure you get a water and not soda because I know how ya'll do!" she spat damn near throwing the cup my way.

"Say bitch, why the fuck you gotta talk to her like that?" I heard a deep voice from behind me. Although he was sticking up for me I frowned at the fact that he called her a bitch. That made him as disrespectful as she was.

"Mannie, don't start shit over here nah. I'm telling you right now that I am not in the fucking mood." She harshly whispered as she checked behind her to see if her manager was near.

"But you in the mood to embarrass people? Don't let that seven twenty-five you make go to your head shawty." He spat back. "Aye ma, get whatever you want and I'll buy it." Looking back, I found the blackest eyes I had ever seen staring back at me.

"No- No thank you." I replied just as my stomach betrayed me and loudly growled. A mug graced his face for a second and then he looked back at the cashier.

"Get me one of every value meal you got and a big ass cup so she can drink all ya'll fucking soda if she wants to. Give us some cookies and pies too." He ordered pulling out a knot of money. After he paid for everything he stepped to the side and against my better judgement I approached him.

"Thank you but I said no thanks." I mumbled.

"Aye hold ya head high and speak up. Don't let no motherfucker put fear in your heart." He told me as his eyes were trained on my face. "Plus, a nigga about to smash most of that with you, I'm higher than giraffe pussy." He said as we both started laughing. Over a bunch of value meals, I spilled my story to a complete stranger. Mannie upgraded my life that day and became the only family I knew until I met Ashleigh. It wasn't until the night before my eighteenth birthday that he fully made me a woman. His woman. The day he left this earth will forever be the saddest day in September.

The ringing of my phone brought me from my thoughts and I was shocked when I realized I was crying. Wiping my face and clearing my throat I answered my phone without even seeing who it was.

"Hello." I answered attempting to clear my throat again because I didn't sound like myself.

"He said he would never hit me again." Ashleigh's voice came through before she started crying uncontrollably. "He fucking lied!"

"Ashleigh what the fuck you mean, he hit you?" I asked running up the stairs and to the cabinet where I grabbed one of Mannie's guns. Mannie was heavy in the streets and made sure that I knew how to protect myself at all times. I was no stranger to gun ranges and had even had to have my man's back in the midst of a shootout. "Ash, calm down and tell me what is going on."

"I just- I just was tired of being a doormat." She started crying again and was able to calm herself down before she continued. "I finally did it Manda. I attempted to stand up to him. He was so drunk and it disgusted me. Before I could stop myself, I snapped. He- He knocked my head against the wall and I must have passed out because I woke up on the kitchen floor. He left me here and just took my car like I meant nothing to him. I just wanna die!" She finished with a cry that shook my spirit. "I don't want to live anymore." She cried over and over. Hearing her saying this broke my heart because I had never heard a woman sound so broken. Grabbing my keys, I was back out the door with my gun riding shotgun.

"Don't say that Ashleigh please?" I damn near begged. "You know how much I love you and I wouldn't know what to do without you. Do me a favor and get dressed, I'll be there in a minute." I said stepping on the gas. I hopped and prayed Dre was there so I could release some aggression on his ass. I listened to her cry but from the movements I heard I knew she was getting ready. Pulling up to her house I noticed her car was still missing so there was no need for me to get down. "I'm outside babe." I said before disconnecting the call and setting some things in motion. I was turning this day around for her. Just as I finished making my arrangements, I saw her walking out. My best friend didn't look like what she had been through but she didn't look like my best friend either.

"I don't need to hear the I told you so speech right now. Maybe later, but just not right now." She said wiping the silent tears that fell as she buckled her seat belt.

"You trust me?" I asked her.

"With my life." She answered.

"Good. Trust that I have your back through whatever and this isn't different. We are heading to Baton Rouge to do some shopping, then New Orleans to do some celebrating. The rest is a surprise, all on me." I watched as shock was evident in her face.

"Amanda, I can't." she said.

"Says who? Yo alcoholic ass free loader? Girl if God is still in the miracle working business that nigga will get sloppy drunk at a bar, try to come home and crash into a fucking tree. I don't wish death on him cause I'm a Christian, but I'll take paralyzed for two hundred Alex. Bitch then we could use him as a punching bag!" I laughed as I merged onto the interstate. Turning up the music, it wasn't long before sleep found Ash and I was lost in my thoughts. She didn't know it but she wouldn't see Louisiana for a week after today. New Orleans was merely a pit stop for us to catch our flight. I was bringing my girl to the concrete jungle, New York. We both needed a getaway. My only hope was the distance was enough for her to leave her problems behind and enjoy life.

Chapter 3

Harlem

"I will probably see you tomorrow. I still have to go get a cut and I want to chill for a minute because knowing Houston I won't get any rest tonight." I told a pouting Kennedy. I already knew she was about to start her begging because her ass never could accept a no.

"You know he just goin have you in some strip club with a stank ass stripper shaking her ass in your face. Why can't we just have a nice quiet dinner together Harlem?" she whined. Running my hand across my face I let out an aggravated breath. I looked around me to check my surrounding before focusing back on my facetime call. When I looked back into the screen she had the camera positioned so that I was getting an eye full of her pretty pink pussy. I immediately rocked up when she stuck her finger in her mouth then inserted it into her pussy. The tattoos crawling up her thick ass thighs ended right where her pussy began. For a second I was jealous of the tattoo artist.

"Damn." I whispered as she stuck a second finger in it and her lips fell into an o formation. Taking her other hand, she grabbed her breast and started pulling at her pierced nipples.

"Baby, wouldn't you rather be here tonight with me?" she asked picking up the pace of her fingers. I licked my lips as I watched her juices drench her fingers then drip down her ass.

"No, the fuck he wouldn't. I'm telling your fucking daddy! I knew you was a freaky lil bit.."

"Houston!" I screamed ending the call and turning to my brother who was at my car window talking through the crack.

"Don't Houston me nigga. You be talking about my girl being a nasty freak and here yo ass go watching that boring shit all early in the morning." He said as I hoped out my jeep wrangler and we shook up. "Nigga we real life too old to still be dressing alike and shit." He laughed as we took in each other's appearance. We were both rocking a Jordan sweat suit with slides. Mine were some Jordan slides and his were Gucci.

"I swear your ass be looking in my window when I'm getting dressed nigga." I laughed back as we walked in the barbershop like we owned that bitch. I mean we really did own it, as well as the beauty salon next door. When we moved to New York three years ago we quickly began putting ourselves in a position to win.

"I know ya'll twins and what not but you do know that dressing alike bullshit gay right?" Kwame laughed as he was shaking up with the both of us. Kwame was a barber here and basically ran the shop. After we decided what we wanted to do with our money it was nothing for us to hit up our cousins Kwame and his sister Toya to run both business. They were back home working in someone else's shop so they jumped on this opportunity.

"Fuck you, pussy. Fuck up my cut and I'll have a big gay nigga waiting at your house for you when you get off." Houston said drawing laughs from everyone in the shop. He jumped in the chair and I made my way to the salon next door. Kwame was the only barber that touched me so I was just going let Toya hook me up with some braids at the top of my head. Normally I rocked my shit in a man bun so I was looking to do something different tonight.

"Heeeeey Harlem." The ladies called out when I walked in. I hit their asses with a head nod and kept it pushing until I got to the back where Toya had her station set up in a private room. She always had some rich and famous client so this was set up to respect their privacy. Knocking on the door I waited for her to answer.

"What's good cousin?" She asked pulling me into a hug.

"Ain't shit, I need you to do something with my head really quick for tonight before your brother hooks me up." I explained.

"You washed it already or you need me to do that too?" She asked grabbing her comb, grease and some liquid shit in a bottle. She knew the routine, I couldn't be in the back room because I needed to see who walked in and out the shop. Though we had legit businesses my brother and I were deep in the streets. When we came here we made a lot of noise and a lot of enemies. The plan was to move in silence but when niggas found out what we were working with our names were ringing louder than church bells. It was no secret that there was some animosity between us and a nigga named Juice. Before we came into the picture I heard he was the nigga to see and now his clients on they Ray Charles shit when it comes to him. Oh well, that nigga fucked up stomping on his shit too much and we lucked up.

"I need you to wash it." I replied knowing I was being ass backwards. I knew I had to go next door and get cut but this would have to do for now. I wanted to get home and relax so I was pressed for time.

"Vontavia, take Harlem to the shampoo bowl and use some of that new product on him please." She asked one of the stylist. I shook my head because anytime I was close to Tavia her ass tried to rape me. We fucked a while back but the pussy was dryer than the Sahara Desert. As if that wasn't enough her ass was too loud. She was screaming and had me feeling like I was raping her ass. I'm blessed as fuck and know what to do with my dick, so I damn sure didn't need her to gas me by making all that noise, which is what I immediately thought she was doing. It wasn't until I brought that shit up when it was Kwame, Houston and I at the crib that I found out the bitch really just couldn't take the dick. I found out them niggas hit her ass too and she acted the same fucking way.

"I got you." She called out to Toya. "And I damn sure got you." She whispered seductively to me. Her plump lips were sexy as fuck with that gloss on them. I instantly thought back to that deadly mouth game she has. She couldn't take the dick in her pussy but her mouth was a different story. Lil mama handled the dick better than super head could on her best day. Thinking of that had a nigga on brick and from the look in her eyes I could tell she saw that shit.

The shampoo bowls were in a separate room also so I wait for her to lead the way. I couldn't help my eyes as they followed the way her ass jiggled with every step. That shit had me forgetting that her pussy was sandpaper dry for a minute. When she looked over her shoulder at me and winked I already knew what time it was. Stepping into the room she held the door open for me and closed and locked it behind me.

"What you doing Tavia, I only came here to get my hair done shawty." I laughed as it fell on deaf ears. She was already tugging my sweatpants and boxers down and holding my dick in her hand like it was the key to the city. I wanted to object because I already knew after head I wanted pussy. I would have stopped her ass if she wasn't looking so right. Vontavia was 12 out of 10 If we weren't counting her pussy and hoe fax. The dress code for the salon was all black and she honored that shit in the sexiest way possible. She was rocking a black fitted dress that hugged her curves like a toddler to his mama. She had a fresh pair of all black huaraches on her feet and her face was bare except for her makeup. She was gorgeous enough to not need that shit. She had this ghetto ass ponytail that fell to the side of her face in curls and hit her waist. It looked good on her.

"I know what you came for and I'm going handle that, but first I'm going handle this. Besides, I wanted to give you a birthday gift." She said before licking up the length of my dick. She took her time making sure she licked every inch of that motherfucker then went to the balls. I moaned like a bitch when she slid my balls into her mouth and jacked my dick off. Grabbing her ponytail, I made her look me in the eyes.

"Stop playing with it and handle this dick." Was all I had to say before she turned into a magician and made my shit disappear down her throat. On God, I went cock eyed in the very moment. Fuck my hair, nothing else matter as she was tightening her jaws on my dick. I felt the saliva from her mouth drip down my shit and then she followed like a vacuum and cleaned that shit up. A nigga almost lost his shit when she took my dick into the back of her throat and snaked her tongue out to lick my balls at the same time. Not being able to control it any longer, I used her throat as a daycare and dropped my kids off. While I sat there with my dick still on hard trying to catch my breath, she went into my wallet and grabbed a condom. Knowing I wanted to slide in something warm I didn't object when she used her mouth to slide it down my dick. Standing up she lifted her dress over her hips and I motioned towards the table that was used for waxing.

"Play in that pussy and get it ready for me." I told her as I stood up beating my dick. I figured maybe her ass could get it wet for me since I couldn't seem to get the job done. I licked my lips as she did the same shit I was just enjoying via facetime steps away from me. When she started moaning I knew she was ready. Grabbing her thighs, I pulled her down so that my dick was positioned at the entrance of her pussy. I rubbed the head of my dick up and down her pussy playing in the lil moisture I felt. I knew not to get to excited because this happened last time. She was moist for about five minutes then that shit went dry.

"Ohhh, stop teasing me and please fuck me Harlem." She moaned completely removing her shirt and freeing the pretties pair of D's I had ever seen. Leaning forward I took her left nipple into my mouth as she moaned. I grabbed the nipple in between my teeth as I slide my dick into her opening. Grabbing her at the waist, I slightly lifted her from the table as I enjoyed the pussy before the inevitable happened. The feeling of my nuts slapping against her ass had a nigga in a trance until I heard screaming. It took a minute before I realized the screaming was coming from her ass. Without a word between the two of us, I pulled out of her, pulled the condom off and pulled my clothes up.

"Wha-what are you doing?" she damn near cried out.

"Ma, I'm not in the business of raping women. You too fucking loud and I'm out. Done gave me a fucking headache." I said on my way out the door.

"Harlem!" She screamed from behind me. I cut her ass off with the slamming of the door.

"You wrong for doing my girl like that." Toya and some of the chicks laughed when I hit the corner.

"Maaaan, I wasn't doing shit. Yo girl do too much bruh. Nah a nigga going have blue balls." I spat mugging her. Her ass knew she sent that girl wash my hair back there knowing what was going to happen.

"You know she has always had a crush on you." She laughed.

"Yeah and on Houston too. Man let me get out of here before she comes out. Meet me at my crib when you leave so you can get me right." I said before jumping in my jeep. My phone started ringing and I know it was Houston wondering where I was going so I ran the story down to him and made plans for Kwame to hook me up at my spot later. Walking into my penthouse I took a minute to enjoy the view of the Hudson River before making my way to the bathroom to shower. The breeze from the door being opened didn't surprise me, I smelled her perfume when I walked in. Turning around I grabbed Kennedy and eased her down onto my throbbing dick. Kennedy was into making love but after the head I got earlier, we were straight fucking.

Chapter 4

Houston

"Something wrong with your brother." Kwame said laughing as I told him what Harlem had just said.

"Ain't shit wrong with twin, you know that broad be screaming her ass off. He just stupid cause his ass ain't peeped game like us. I know when I go over there to go prepared for her ass." I said pulling out a drawer behind Kwame's desk and pulling out the tube of KY Jelly.

"Nigga, something wrong with your ass too. When you stashed that shit here?" He asked laughing.

"The day after I caught Leah with that bum ass nigga. I'm used to getting pussy at least every other day so I been knocking her shit out the frame, every other fucking day. I'm waiting on her to walk her bowlegged ass back in the shop now so I can go over there and put the pussy in a sarcophagus. I already know she took her ass to her apartment up the block and took a shower." I said knowing she was a neat freak. A few minutes after Harlem shot out, so did she.

"Shit you could have just grabbed the bottle that I keep at her station. After work when she in the shop cleaning I knock her down before I go home." He said making me laugh. We in this bitch talking like some hoes on the same female. We don't speak on none of the other broads we are hitting, cause that ain't got shit to do with the other. But Vontavia ass was community property. I ain't never fucked behind my brother or Kwame and vice versa so when we found out we all had her at some capacity that was supposed to be it. Lil mama made it hard as hell to leave her alone though. True enough she would never be wifey material but she wasn't someone you just quit either. I never kissed the hoe on neither set of lips, but when you find a bitch that makes you tap out from head alone then you keep her around. I don't even allow another bitch to give me head because they can't touch her skills and that shit just ends up pissing me off. I had left her alone for like two weeks when she approached me. I had come here to look over the paperwork and one of the chicks that used to work next door came in talking about she could help me. I thought she meant the paperwork but she had something else in mind. I should have known shit was going to go left when she hesitated after pulling out my dick but I let her do her.

Between listening to her complain that her mouth hurt, coaching her on how to suck my dick and telling her about watching her teeth my dick went to sleep on her ass. I wasted no time kicking her out with no excuse. The fuck I need to give an excuse for? Her ass knew what she did wrong. When I heard the door open again I thought she was back but instead Vontavia stood in the doorway in a pair of black tights and a crop top. I couldn't focus on anything else but how her pussy print was on full display. I was crazy for a fat pussy and I was backed up and ready to bust a nut or two or four. Leaning back into the chair I didn't have to ask why she was there. My dick was already out so she walked over and got to work. She didn't even object when I pulled out the KY Jelly and fuck the lining out of her pussy on the desk. She was always loud as fuck but unlike my twin I didn't give a fuck. She could have been mute and I was still going to get me. After that, I fucked her whenever I felt the need to. I wasn't trying to marry her so I could give a fuck who else she fucked.

"There she go in them lil ass shorts." Kwame said snapping me from my thoughts as Vontavia passed in front of the big window of the shop. She turned and ran her tongue over her lips before pulling her bottom one in between her teeth. All I could do was shake my head and laugh. Her ass thought she was stringing Kwame and I along because she thought we didn't know about the other fucking. WRONG! We just didn't give a fuck.

"I'm out." I said as I pocketed the lube, then walked through the door that led into the salon. Before I could make it all the way inside, I felt a hand grab mine. Although I was being led down the hallway and saw just her backside, I would know that ass from anywhere. Watching the sway of her hips had me more than ready to break her back in.

"I knew you would be on the way over here as soon as I saw you." Vontavia damn near moaned in my ear once we walked into the shampoo room.

31

"Shit if you knew I was coming you should have already been on your knees waiting on me to slide my dick in between those lips." I said pulling my dick out and letting her do what she was best at. After allowing her to drain a nigga I caught a breath or two before I put it down something proper. "Aye get on your knees on that chair. Put your head in the shampoo bowl and I swear on my last nut if you make all that fucking noise you goin be finding Nemo." I warned before sliding on a condom and making sure her pussy was drenched with lubricant. I felt her pussy expanding around my dick as I slide in until I was balls deep.

"Ooooh Houston." She moaned lightly. I pulled all the way out until just my head was still in before I slowly eased my way back into her pussy. I don't know what magic she had worked down there but I swear she was virgin tight and I knew not one of her walls was anything close to a virgin. That pussy had me wanting to cry out when she tightened her muscles.

WHAP!

"You biting the shit out of my dick." I said as I watched her ass jiggle from the slap I laid on it. Knowing I was about to write my name all in this pussy I grabbed one of the towels used to dry off hair and stuffed it in her mouth. As soon as I made sure her has couldn't make all that noise I went in for the kill. I started hitting her with strokes that were so deep and quick that it sounded like a slow clap in this bitch. Even with a towel in her mouth I clearly heard the bitch screaming my name. I was too close to nutting to quit at this point so I literally drowned her ass out. Not missing a stroke, I turned the cold water on in the shampoo bowl and held her fucking head down. She had me fucked up with all that noise. The water wasn't on high so her ass wouldn't die. She tried to get up from under the sink but that was just making her throw that ass back on my dick and like a wide receiver I was catching that shit. The freak started moaning like I didn't have her head under all that damn water. I felt her body shudder as she came and I was right behind her. Pulling out I ripped off the condom and sprayed my seeds all over her fat ass.

"I can't believe you did that to me Houston!" She screamed once she was able to breathe like herself again.

"Shit I don't know why the fuck not. I told you what would happen if you started all that fucking noise again. Messing with yo ass, you goin fuck around and make one of these bitches in here call the cops on me and shit. I'm out." I said pulling up my clothes and leaving her ass there pissed off but satisfied. I didn't want to run into Toya so I went back through the side door and made it to my car. Knowing we was going fuck up the scene tonight I drove home to shower then straight to the mall so I could fuck up some commas.

****

"Nigga, you stay in the mall longer than some bitches I know." Kwame complained as usual. I didn't tell this nigga to come meet me so he could leave whenever he was ready to.

"But yo ass knew that before you invited yourself." I said to him before turning to the bad ass female working at foot locker. She was trying to flirt from the moment we walked in but shorty looked like she just made 18, if that. I like my freedom more than I liked pussy and a nigga ain't never been a pedophile. "Aye, shawty let me get a 10 in these." I said holding up the olive-green huaraches.

"That's all you need?" she questioned in her deep New York accent. I had her ass running back and forward to that backroom but I don't understand why she cared, I was buying all these bitches.

"You recommend anything else?" I asked.

"Well you can't go wrong with a pair of timbs." She suggested.

"Yeah, I see ya'll rock them bitches tough out here. They ain't really me but grab yourself a pair." I said as she smiled.

"Seriously?" she confirmed.

"Yeah, handle that. I'm ready to go." I said going to the register. As I waited for her to return with my shoes I looked into the food court and immediately got pissed off. Leah bitch ass sat in the food court with that pussy ass nigga Krit. Leah was my everything at one point. When we move to New York she came with me and shit was good. It wasn't until I was playing with the cameras in my spot and came across a video of her fucking some nigga in my bed did that shit end. I was Leah's first so I damn sure thought I had the pussy on lock. The joke was on me when the bitch made an extra key for the enemy. Krit was one of the niggas we had knocked off the top when we moved her and now his ass was struggling. They could struggle together because I let that bitch roam like Wi-Fi.

"Damn, Leah look basic as fuck now." Kwame said as he and the chick walked up with my shoes. All I could do was nod my head in agreeance. I was all for a woman in her natural state but that wasn't Lea style. She loved to be decked out in all the best and she rocked the expensive ass foreign hair when we were together. When I kicked her out I made sure she left all my shit right where it was. Today her ass looked like a Rainbow special and she looked like she was in dire need of a salon. Paying for my things I made my way to the exit but I had to pass through the food court where they were sharing a meal. My feet had its own mind as I walked towards their table.

"I wonder if ya'll trying to be romantic by sharing a meal or that stash dried up." I said standing over them. Their reactions were completely different although they noticed me at the same time. A look of sadness flashed across Leah's face and a mug was on Krit's face. "What's up Leah."

"Fuck you nigga, get the fuck from around me and my bitch. She ain't allowed to talk to fuck niggas." He said wrapping his arm around Leah.

"She fucks and lay on side of a fuck nigga nightly and you worried about her saying wassup to a boss. Nigga you and her should know that once she gave the pussy to you chances of me sliding back in her was slimmer than a white ballerina. You will never brag that we had the same bitch." I laughed.

"Oh, but we did have the same bitch. And in the same fucking bed at that." He spat wiping the smile from my face.

"It's cause your broke ass couldn't afford to even get her a room. I understand your back was against the wall. I ain't tripping though because I gave that spot to the cleaning lady and upgraded myself." I told him before speaking to her. "Ma you never knew that a bum ain't supposed to get a diamond, he wouldn't know what to do with that shit. When you were with me you looked like a diamond and now yo ass looking like something from the beauty supply store. Get y'all selves something nice and come show me and my twin some love tonight." I said before popping the band off of a roll and making it rain on them. Leah didn't even look shocked she knew I was a flashy ass nigga that was with the shits. I saw the mug that graced Krit's face and fixed my hand in a gun and made a motion like I pulled the trigger. That nigga time was shorter than them bitches on little women.

Chapter 5

Ashleigh

"Bitch if you don't get your ass home in the next five minutes you will regret ever leaving!" I listened to yet another threatening message from Dre and clicked 7 to delete this one like I had done the others.

"Girl why don't you just block his ass!" Amanda said rolling her eyes as we sat enjoying our pedicures.

"I already know when I get back there will be hell to pay. Blocking him will only make it worse. I'm just going to power it back off." I said doing just that for the fifth time since we landed in New York. When I woke up on a plane I wanted to kill Amanda. When she told me how I ended up on a plane without my knowledge, I tried to kill her. Her ass got me drunk, slipped me a sleeping pill then had some strange man carry me on the plane. Her ass had the nerve to give him my number so when I woke up on the flight he was all smiles the whole time. Homeboy really thought he had something in me. Wrong! After turning up in New Orleans last night I thought that was it for my fun and we would stay the night then head home. I wouldn't have been opposed to that plan, I really had a blast. She kept the drinks coming and I kept knocking them back. I had even danced on a couple of men and really just let my hair down for the first time in forever.

"Umm Ash, powering off your phone is pointless if yo ass just goin turn it back on and listen to the messages." She mumbled closing her eyes and enjoying the massage that the chair was giving her. Leaning back and closing my eyes, my mind drifted off. I knew I had so much to do to accomplish my goals and Dre would just hold me back. I know I needed to get rid of him but I already knew that would be easier said than done. Feeling eyes on me I looked up and saw Amanda studying my facial expression.

"What is there something on my face?" I asked.

"Yep, a frown. You were thinking about your sorry sack of shit huh?" She asked guessing correctly.

"Whatever, I was actually thinking of where to begin." I half lied.

"Where to begin what?" She questioned.

"Like now that I have my degree in hand, what do I do next? I mean I know what to do but it seems like it's so fucking much." I vented. "I haven't even saved money for a location for my salon. How can I when I'm carrying the whole household on my back?"

"I know you're tired of me telling you to get rid of Dre but bitch do just that. Your bills wouldn't be as high as they are if his ass wasn't home all day soaking up your air and using your lights." She preached.

"Amanda!" I warned. I know she was speaking the truth but I didn't want to hear that right now.

"Alright, alright. I'll make a deal with you. I will pay the first three months of your lease once you find the spot for your salon." She said causing me to have a bipolar reaction. I wanted to smile and cry at the same time because I wanted to say yes but I had no idea what her half of the bargain was.

"Nah bruh. I don't want it!" I answered as she fell out laughing. My toes were finally polished so I waited for the lady to slide my flip flops on and made my way to the table so I could dry. Moments later, Amanda joined me.

"You didn't even let me finish." She said laughing.

"Nah cause see yo ass is always on some bullshit. You goin have me doing ignorant shit for that money." I said shaking my head no.

"I swear I'm not. All I ask is that you actually enjoy yourself here. Go with the flow of things, whatever happens you let it happen! Forget about Dre and forget that we are only here for a week. Can you do that?" She asked. This seemed too good to be true.

"Hell ye-" I started

"Nah don't just say yeah to say yeah. You can't be stuck up and I damn sure don't want to hear you saying you are taken." She said making me think before I answered. What the fuck did I really have to lose?

"Yeah, I can do that." I answered not knowing that I made a deal with the devil.

Trenae

****

"Bitch! You are wearing the fuck out of that dress!" Amanda screamed as I ran my hands along my dress to knock out any wrinkles.

"You think? My hips look huge in this shit." I said tugging along the bottom of the royal blue dress. The dress fit me like a glove and I am almost sure if you looked close enough that you would see my heart beating. The only thing stopping this dress from being painted on was the thin lace thong I wore. It really did no good because my ass swallowed it whole as soon as I slid it on. My breast sat just right in this dress so there was no need for a bra. The only accessories I wore were the diamond studs in my ear and the Giuseppe Zanotti booties that were stealing the show. I was eyeing them in the store but knew I didn't have three stacks to drop on some shoes. Imagine my surprise when Amanda pulled out a pair for her and me when we got to the room. I couldn't stop looking at them as I walked. Jennifer Lopez, know she fucked it up when she designed these.

"Chile your hips are huge. You say that like it's a bad thing. Baby you are thicker than some of my grand mama's grits. And trust me those bitches were thick." Amanda said standing up from her makeshift vanity after beating her face. She had done mine before I went get dressed and now all I had to do was remove the flexi rods from my bundles. She

40

decided to slick her hair down and it sat in the nape of her neck in a long silky ponytail.

"You wanna put on some clothes bitch?" I acted as if I was vomiting at the sight of her standing in just her black boy shorts. Truth be told, Amanda was stacked. Her chocolate skin always had a golden glow to it and I had always told her she should model because she was so beautiful. She was talking about I was thick and true I was thicker than she was, but her thickness sat just on her hips and ass.

"Bitch you know I have you thinking about how you can get in between these thighs." She joked flicking her tongue at me and dropping it low. After a few more jokes she stepped into a jumpsuit that was made with her in mind. It was a halter top made of thin material with shiny strands of material all over it. If it wasn't for the boy shorts she wore there would be nothing left to the imagination. Her breast stood at attention and you could visibly see her nipples. "Let's snap it up for the gram and then we can dip." She said right before we had a mini photoshoot then hopped in our awaiting car.

The uber driver had some Jay Z blasting so we were turning up in the car with him. It was still funny when we would get weird looks from these New Yorkers because of our friendly disposition. Everyone from down south knows that greeting people and smiling is like second nature for us and here they just think you are weird. The driver initially thought the same thing but as soon as we started spitting the Jay Z lyrics he was team us. We pulled up to the club and was easily granted access after one long ass eye rape from the bouncer.

"Don't forget your part of the deal." Amanda reminded me as we made our way to the bar to get some drinks in our system. "Let me get eight shots of patron with limes." She ordered.

"Ummm, who the fuck is drinking all that shit?" I asked looking at her like she was nuts.

"Three months of rent says we are!" she said as they were placed in front of us. Without a second thought, we each took four and threw them back like professionals.

"I think I'm in love." I heard from behind me causing Amanda and I to spin around only to be face to face with either a set of twins or brothers that looked freakishly alike. "Damn, I mean you gorgeous but you really fucked up my view." One of them said to Amanda as he drank from a bottle of Ace of Spades.

"How you doing shawty, my name is Harlem." The other said getting close to my ear so he could be heard over the music.

"I'm t…" I started but felt a nudge from Amanda reminding me of the deal I had made. "If you are Harlem, then I'm Brooklynn." I replied throwing caution to the wind. I extended my hand to shake and he pulled me in for a hug. "Ma, it's my birthday I ain't settling for no handshake." He replied kissing me on my jawline. I could smell the liquor on his breathe and the gloss in his eyes let me know he was full.

"Your birthday huh?" I questioned as he looked at me like I was a buffet and he was starving.

"Yeah so you gotta be extra nice to me." When I felt his arm ease lower down my back and comfortably sit on the top of my ass I didn't jump or move his hand like I normally would. In fact, I actually leaned into him.

"Where I'm from we don't talk to strangers." I flirted back.

"Shit, I'm not a stranger. I'm Harlem and you Brooklyn." He said before we were interrupted.

"Aye ya'll remember we were still standing here, right? Ya'll gazing into each other's eyes like ya'll don't see us here. Got me dealing with this rude broad and shit." His brother said.

"And this fool is my twin brother Houston." Harlem introduced him.

"Wait a minute, my nigga did you just call me a rude broad?" Amanda asked snapping in his face.

"Fuck, I call that shit like I see it." He said back before taking another swig of his drink. I knew Amanda was on her level when she snatched the bottle from his mouth and placed it between her lips before turning it up.

"Now, you can call me a rude bitch." She said before walking off like a model with his bottle. Houston's mouth was open as he watched her strut off.

"Nigga I think I want her to be my first ex-wife and baby mama." He told Harlem before following after her. I started to head that way before his grip tightened around my waist.

"Why you trying to leave a nigga lonely on his birthday ma?" He whispered in my ear.

"You in a club full of people and you screaming that you lonely." I replied.

"Yeah but those people ain't here for me ma. I'm only worried about you. Let me get you a drink." He said. I couldn't help but laugh when he spun me around and allowed me to lead the way to the bar. Looking back his eyes was glued on my ass so I made sure I put a lil extra sway in my hips. After being around Dre who did nothing but insult my thickness, it felt good for someone to make me feel sexy. Stopping at the bar I felt him press himself against my ass and was pleasantly surprised to feel the monster he was working with was awake.

"See what you done with all that ass you had swinging from side to side? What you goin do about that?" He asked in my ear again. I knew the effects of those shots had took over because without a second thought I answered.

"If I wrapped it in wrapping paper, put a bow on top of it and addressed it to Harlem, you wouldn't know what to do with all this." I replied taking his hand and placing it on my ass, allowing him to grab a handful. I didn't think it was possible but his dick grew harder.

"Keep playing ma and you'll end my lil birthday get together before the clock strikes midnight." He said as the bartender approached us. "Let me get her some fruity shit that ain't to strong." He said making me side eye him. I was far from a drinker but I refused to let him think I was some lightweight.

"Nah baby, he can have that fruity shit." I replied. I couldn't think of a strong drink and had to keep up my facade now so I said the first thing that came to mind. "Let me get 8 shots of patron and limes."

"Damn ma you turning up like that?" He joked.

"Nah we are turning up like that." I said sliding the four shots in front of him and taking my four. "To you." I said raising one.

"Nah ma, to the queen wearing the fuck out of that blue dress." He said lifting his glass then throwing shot after shot back. Not to be outdone, I followed suit. I looked around for Amanda but couldn't see anything because of the thickness of the crowd.

"Did you see where they went?" I asked Harlem who was staring in my face.

"They probably in our section ma. Let's go." He said grabbing my hand and leading me to a VIP section That was halfway filled with people. It didn't take me long to find Amanda but I damn sure was shocked to see her straddling Houston and sucking on his lips. You would have sworn they had been fucking with each from how comfortable they were.

Both of Houston's hands had a handful of ass in each and Amanda had her long legs wrapped around his waist as they sat on the couch.

"Shit I see they have you two looking just like I was. One minute they were fussing and lil mama was letting him have it and the next he picked her ass off her feet and tongues her down. I thought for sure she would mix on his ass but she just wrapped her legs around them. They asses been like that since." Some guy with the sexiest dark skinned I had ever laid eyes on said walking up. He was handsome and had the most beautiful hair I had ever seen on a man.

"Kwame this is Brooklyn. I know that ain't her real name but she wanna play and shit. Brooklyn this my cousin Kwame. That chick over there dancing on the couch all ratchet like is his sister Toya." He said pointing at a bad ass female that was killing some over the knee peep toe booties and an all in one short set that had to be custom made.

"Wassup Brooklyn. You know you need to stop lying to my boy. Yo ass don't look like no damn Brooklyn." He said laughing.

"Well what does a Brooklyn look like?" I questioned.

"Shit all the Brooklyn's I met were hood as the fuck. You look like a Jessica, a Rachael or an Ashley." He hit the nail on the head.

"Ugh, I couldn't have a boring name like Ashley. I would have to spice it up if that was my name. Like a different spelling from the norm or something."

"Yeah alright, I'll figure that out. I can't have just anyone around my cousin." He said showing off a row of perfectly white teeth.

"I'm not just anyone, I'm Brooklyn." I finished as my song came on. I was in my zone swaying my hips to the beat and signing until Harlem slicked the fuck out of me.

"All these bitches, but my eyes on you. Is you somebody's baby? If you ain't, girl, what we gon' do?" He sang in my ear. This nigga could real life sing too. In the middle of this club I wanted to remove my thongs and hand them to him.

"Dear God, forgive me. If this man sets it up I guarantee you that I'm leaving the club with him and giving him the birthday gift he will never forget." I thought to myself as he continued singing in my ear. When Nicki part came on I know his ass may have thought I was going to sing it but that was a lie. I couldn't sing to save my life so I just continue winding my hips on him.

"Y'all look all lovey dovey." I heard and looked up into Amanda's eyes.

"I know you ain't talking. For a second I didn't know where your lips ended and Houston's began." I laughed as the section filled with bottle girls with bottles and sparkles. A cake was rolled out in the shape of Two H's and Two chains birthday song started playing. After blowing out their candles the bottles were in rotation and everyone was just vibing. Houston and Amanda had found another corner before a chick approached them. Baby girl looked like she was with the drama so I made my way over with Harlem behind me.

"Who is she?" I asked as we walked over.

"Leah. She and Houston have history." Was all he said. I walked up just as Houston told her get lost but she didn't seem to happy. As if she wasn't standing there he and Amanda were right back sucking each other's lips.

"In my fucking face though Houston? Why would you invite me here if you would bring her?" She screamed. I watched as Amanda ended their kiss and addressed Leah without facing her. In fact, she was wiping her lipstick off of Houston's lips and giving him googily eyes.

"Look bitch, he invited you to the club and you're here at the club. The fuck else you want him to do? You want a bottle or something? Here!" she said grabbing a bottle from the table and pushing it in front of Leah. "Now go about your fucking business. Bitch we in a club so fucking mingle." She spat.

"You can calm down with all the bitches. This is between Houston and I!" She spat back

"Only thing between you and Houston is me hoe! You would want to move around before I make you move around. Matter of fact, I'm faded and feeling x rated." She said

"Oh, it's Mr. Nasty time!" Houston finished as they fell out laughing. A defeated Leah stepped off. "Shit all bullshit to the side we can go if you on that level." He said. Without a single word, she got off his lap and stood up while motioning

48

for him to lead the way. As he stepped off to dap his boys up Amanda made her way to me.

"You so foul for leaving me hoe." I joked.

"If you don't want me to go I won't go. You know you come first." She said.

"Nah you can go ahead with Houston, she with me." Harlem answered causing me to shrug.

"Yeah, I'm with him." I said and for once Dre was not affecting my decision.

Chapter 6

Harlem

Rolling over last night's events were fuzzy due to the hangover I was suffering with. I don't know what hyped my ass up to drink so heavy knowing the consequences. I was never a drinker, I would rather smoke on some loud and play the background. All the drinking and partying was some shit that Houston and Kwame enjoyed. The ringing from my phone wasn't helping my headache so I searched for it without opening my eyes until my hands landed on something that was not my phone.

"Harlem get your hand off my ass." The person mumbled. Instantly memories of Brooklyn flooded through my head. Remembering how fine she was last night made me open my eyes and flip the covers off of her to take another look. The mug that graced her face when she popped up was sexy as shit. I couldn't focus on that when I realized that she was topless and only wearing a thong. Her titties were sitting just right, not perfect but just right for her. They had some weight to them so no they weren't perky, but they were far from saggy. For a moment last night, I thought that one of those corset things was the cause of her perfect hourglass silhouette but here she was looking better than she did last night.

"Damn." I said aloud noticing the tent I was causing.

"Nah, it's way too late for your mans to want to wake up now. Last night I thought yo ass had E.D." she said putting her face back in the pillow.

"The fuck is E.D?" I asked mugging her because that shit sounded like some type of sexually transmitted disease.

"Erectile Dysfunction." She answered rolling to her side and propping her hand under her head. Her hair fell over her face and she threw it back and met my gaze.

"I know that better not be what I think it is?" I said. Using motherfucking context clues I know she was saying something about my erections being dysfunctional.

"It means either your dick won't get hard, won't stay hard long or your ass just don't have the desire to fuck." She explained with a shrug.

"What the fuck you mean? You see this shit?" I asked flipping the covers back and grabbing my dick that was semi hard and laying on my thigh. "This grade A beef ma and it surely gets harder than Chinese arithmetic and stays that way until the motherfucking job is done. As for my desire to fuck..." I trailed off as I jumped up and grabbed her by her thigh causing her to lay flat on her back. I ignored the shocked yelp that escaped from her lips. Fuck her shock, I was about to show lil mama that a nigga didn't have a big dick for show. She tried to squeeze her thighs together but I effortlessly ripped them apart then did the same to her thong.

"Harlem, wait!" Came from one set of lips but the wetness that I observed from her other set of lips had a nigga wanting to ignore her ass. My dick was so hard it was literally paining me not to bury it deep in her fat pussy.

"Ma, don't do that. Pleeeaaassse, don't do that?" I damn near begged as I rubbed the tip of my dick against her pussy lips. My head immediately started gleaming from the moisture that coated her pussy lips. Despite her asking me to wait her eyes tightened and she bit her lip in anticipation. Positioning my dick at her entrance I lightly pushed the tip of my dick into her folds and enjoyed the tightness.

"Noooo, please." She moaned. Her lips were saying stop but the way her pussy was gripping my dick felt like a green light. Despite how right this shit felt, the lady said no so I stepped back and removed my dick from what I know could be its new home. I looked as her cheeks reddened and she composed herself then quickly sat up in the bed. Even the site of her breast bouncing couldn't distract me from wanting to plunge all ten inches into her dripping pussy.

"Ma, what you doin? Why you asked me to stop?" I questioned stroking my dick to relieve some of the ache.

"Harlem, I can't. Last night I was on another level and wanted to do nothing more than ride your dick until my legs cramped up." She explained never removing her eyes from my dick. I could have sworn I saw her ass drool a little. Without another thought, I walked out the room into the sitting room area and grabbed a few bottles of that little ass liquor from the refrigerator. Walking back in the room with my dick leading the way I tossed them shits on the bed.

"Well let's replay last night. Drink that shit and get on that level right quick." I said dead ass serious.

"Harrrllleeeemmmm." She pleaded for my understanding.

"Yeah man. Let me go handle this, I'll be back." I said pointing to my dick and walking to the rest room. I know she probably thought I was pissed off and I was, just not at her. Fuck, don't no nigga enjoy getting his dick ready for some pussy only not to get any. Taking a piss helped relieve some pressure so I started the shower, hopped in and jacked my shit off. I'm a grown ass man so I knew how to handle this until I was able to slide in something warm and wet. After finishing then washing of I wrapped a towel around my waist then walked out to a sight that almost made that shit a waste. Baby girl was on the floor under the bed, all I saw was all that ass tooted up in the air. I had to tell my junior to chill out and sit down cause he was ready to stand up at attention again. I was both happy and pissed she slid her dress back on. Happy because if all that ass was bare then I don't know if I could control myself. Mad because the arch in her back was perfect and I'm sure the sight would be so much better minus the clothing.

"Where the fuck is my phone, Dre goin kill me." She mumbled to herself as she continued her search. "Fuck man!" she said coming from under the bed. When she noticed, me she jumped a little but nothing too serious. I wanted to see if her ass was on some sneak shit.

"Who is Dre?" I asked not because I was jealous but because I wanted to see if she would keep it real.

"Oh, you heard that. He's my problem." She said while shrugging. I saw the sadness in her eyes when I brought up his name.

"Your man?" I asked for clarification.

"No, my grown ass boy. Dre and man shouldn't be used in the same sentence." She explained before changing the subject. "I'm sorry about earlier."

"No need to apologize. I respect you for telling me no. Shit I don't even know your real name." I laughed as she rolled her eyes.

"I told you my name was Brooklyn." She lied again.

"Alright, I'll take that for now. Not that I'm complaining, why were you in my bed and you got a man ma?" I asked. I watched as her face frowned up and she thought before she spoke.

"Look, I told you I don't have a man. I have a boy in a man's body. Dre is a situation that I want to shake. I came here to have fun for the next six days and forget I know Dre. Thank you for last night, I had a great time." She said standing to her feet and grabbing her shoes and her purse. For some reason, I didn't want her to go. I couldn't explain it because a nigga never aspired to play the side nigga role but that's not what spilled from my lips when I opened my mouth.

"If you had a great time last night imagine what I can make of your remaining six days." I said before I thought of what I was saying. I watched as confusion flashed in her eyes before she squinted and tilted her head.

"What are you saying?" she asked.

"Let me be the person that you spend the next six days with ma. If you want to forget that nigga exist for a week, let me help you." I said sounding like a Keith Sweat as nigga. I don't give a fuck what nobody was thinking, I was far from soft but she just felt right. I needed to get to know her, even if only for one week.

"Why?" she asked. "Don't get me wrong, I know I'm pretty and I know my body is desirable." As soon as she said that it made me want to take back my offer. I don't need another Kennedy and that's what she was sounding like. Kennedy ass was so full of herself and all she had to offer was her looks. I almost said just that until she finished speaking. "But, I'm not beat on my looks. And I'm lonely so I won't be offering ass just to be in your presence." She said dropping her purse and shoes and sticking her hands on her hips.

"Ma, I'm not hard up for ass. Something just feels right about you." I confessed hoping she wouldn't look at me as some tender dick ass nigga. She chewed on her bottom lip before she picked up her belongings and headed to the door. I wasn't about to chase a female so I shrugged it off as she opened the door.

"I'm going to my room and shower. You better show me the time of my life." She said over her shoulder before closing the door.

Chapter 7

Ashleigh

I couldn't front like I didn't know what Harlem was talking about. He felt like comfort. If I had to explain it, it would be like getting off of work after a long tiresome day then bathing and laying down on fresh sheets. Don't act like that isn't one of the best feelings ever! Last night was a lil fuzzy but I could remember a bit of what happened and I was embarrassed. After Amanda and Houston left we kicked it for a bit in the club and continued drinking. I knew I was past my limit and should have stopped but like I said, I was comfortable with him. After a few too many shots we got an uber and couldn't keep our hands off of each other. Not once was I worried about Dre or Louisiana for that matter.

We decided to get a room at the same hotel Amanda and I were already staying at since I assumed she and Houston went to our room. The ride up the elevator was filled with us tonguing each other down and him gripping my ass. We had even gone, as far as him sliding his fingers under my dress, sliding my thong to the side and fingering me while a couple were on the elevator with us. I remember biting my lip so my moans wouldn't escape. I was on my Janet Jackson shit and wanted him anytime and anyplace. I real life didn't give a fuck who was around. If the elevator hadn't stopped on our floor when it did I would have hiked up my dress, grabbed my ankles and we would have given that old ass couple a show. It would have been ass smacking and hair grabbing like we were alone. It was too late for their old asses to be out anyway. Getting to the room, I just knew I was going to get fucked so good I would need physical therapy to walk again and I welcomed it. Imagine my surprise when I went to the bathroom to freshen up and walked out in just my thong to this nigga snoring. Thinking all he needed was a wake-up call I undressed him and popped his dick in my mouth. Thinking back, I had to be lit because I had only sucked dick once and hated it. Yet here I was with a big yet soft dick in my mouth. I probably looked like I was getting my temperature taken with a big ass thermometer. I gave up and fell the fuck to sleep when I realized he wasn't waking up. If I said I didn't want to fuck him silly without the liquid courage I would be lying. I needed to deny him so I wouldn't feel like a hoe but I wanted him to ignore my ass and pass go while collecting two hundred dollars.

I didn't waked up with any regrets today though. I mean, why should I? This didn't even have anything to do with the deal between Amanda and me. I think getting away from Dre allowed me to see clearly for once. I didn't want nor need Dre and I knew what I needed to do when I got back. The fear of an ass whipping was still in the back of my mind, especially since I lost my phone and knew he had been blowing me up.

What made me not worry about that fear was the determination I was feeling. I was going with my move when I got home and I'm going with my move with Harlem. This didn't feel like cheating because as far as I knew it, I was single. Harlem offering to show me a good time while I was here was music to my ears. I wanted to feel desired by a man again and I hoped that he was the man for the job. Getting to my room, I slide my card and entered but wish I hadn't.

"Ooooh fuck me harder Houston. Fuck me with that big dick!" I heard Amanda moan out as she threw her ass back on a naked Houston. The only thing this nigga was wearing was his chains that were slapping against his bare chest. I know I should look away but I'm nasty as fuck. I loved watching porn and here I was watching live porn. Watching Amanda slid up the length of his dick and throw her ass back had me in a trance. My bitch was handling that dick and trust me he was far from small. Their appearance wasn't the only thing Houston and Harlem shared, they were both packing with no destination in mind. I watched as Houston slapped her ass and her brown skin turned red. The slap must have done it for her because she was squirting moments later and Houston pulled out and emptied his babies all on her ass.

"Damn bitch, you goin teach me how to squirt like that?" I asked dead ass serious as they both jumped and looked in my direction. Houston didn't have a shy bone in his body because his ass didn't try to hide his semi erect dick.

"Wassup ma." He nodded his head then laid in the bed like this shit was normal. "I'm sure Harlem can help you with that." He laughed. Amanda threw the covers on him as she stood to her feet.

"Bitch how long you been there?" she asked laughing. We had seen each other naked more times than I could count so of course she wasn't running to cover up.

"Girl I came too late, that shit ended about two minutes after I came in. This was better than watching xnxx with surround sound." I laughed. "Nah but I have to ask you something after you wipe that man seeds off yo ass." I said and like she forgot it was there she ran to the bathroom to do just that.

"Aye, where bro at?" Houston asked still breathing funny.

"Up the hall." I replied before turning to grab my luggage. Everything that was packed in the closet I just grabbed the hangers and laid them across the couch area.

"Umm, where you going?" Amanda asked walking back in.

"Well at first I was going to come in here and beg you to understand before you go mad." I started. "But then I realized your time may be occupied anyway. Harlem wants me to spend the week with him. He wants to show me a good time." I explained.

"And you actually want to go with him?" she questioned.

"Yeah, I do" I shocked myself by admitting with no hesitation. "I really do." I repeated with a smile.

"Let me check your temperature." She said with her hand extended to feel my forehead and I smacked it away.

"Oh no hoe, I have no idea where that hand was." I laughed. "Let me go brush my teeth and grab my things from the bathroom." I said setting everything down and bypassing her. Looking in the mirror of the bathroom I smiled at my appearance. I had a little glow to me. You know that you don't just glow from pregnancy and bomb dick right. I had a fuck by free glow, even if it was just temporary. I quickly brushed and flossed my teeth before grabbing all my personal items. Stepping out the bathroom I had to laugh at Houston and Amanda. Their asses knew I hadn't left the suite but they were fucking like they were alone. This time she was riding his ass into the sunset. Of course, my nasty ass watched and noticed he didn't have a condom on. I hoped my girl knew she was tap dancing on thin ice. Before I could step away her ass spun around with his dick still inside of her and started riding him reverse cowgirl. Houston was moaning like a bitch as he gripped her waist and thrust upward to match her stride. As if she was merely sitting on a chair she spoke with no problems.

"Be safe and keep me updated on your whereabouts. OOOOOHHHHHH SHIIITTTT! Remember our deal. FUCCCCKKKKK HOUSTON. And have fun. YAAASSSS RIGHT THE FUCK THERE." I shook my head as this bitch spoke to me while she was cumin on the dick.

"Yeah and bye." I said grabbing my things and running out the room. I didn't even have the time to tell her I lost my phone. I power walked to Harlem's room and bang on the door until he swung it open still wearing just his towel.

"What's wrong?" he asked me as he looked from side to side in the hallway.

"Nothing, I need to shower." I said pushing past him with my luggage and rushing to the bathroom. Putting the water on a warm temperature I stripped then hopped in. Watching Amanda and Harlem had me hot and bothered. Way more then I cared to admit so that was the rush to the shower. Sitting on the bench that was in the back of the shower, I leaned against the wall and placed one foot in the area for the bar soap before inserting two fingers into my pussy. It was already dripping wet and that had nothing to do with the water cascading down on my naked frame. Grinding into my fingers I closed my eyes and moaned out knowing the water would drown out the sounds. I was so into what I was doing that I didn't pay attention to the knocking on the door. I didn't pay attention to the door knob turning. I was so close to my peak that I didn't pay attention to Harlem walking into the rest room and abandoning his towel. I didn't even notice him when his fingers replaced mine. I was in a zone and knew that my end was near. It wasn't until the fingers were remove and replaced with a tongue did I snap back into reality. Opening my eyes, I was staring back into Harlem's deep brown ones. How didn't I notice him enter the shower and drop to his knees?

"Harlem, no…" I started before he cut me off by inserting the same fingers that were just inside of me into my mouth. Like I was trained by this man I started sucking on them.

"I just want to help you out. We won't fuck until you want us to." He said, tone filled with lust before filling his mouth with my pussy. The feeling that I was feeling was incomparable. Dre never gave my head and he was my first so this was foreign to me. There is no way in a hell a tongue in my pussy should feel so amazing. The way Harlem's eyes were gazing into my own heightened the experience. I was seeing rainbows, unicorns and clouds as this man took my body on an adventure with just his mouth and his tongue. There was a warm tingling feeling that I felt build up in the center of my being that erupted right into Harlem's mouth and he happily slurped it up. I didn't understand why his body was convulsing like I was until I watched as his thick nut rinsed towards the drain. The thought to repay him flashed into my mind but as promised, he helped me out then stepped out of the shower.

Chapter 8

Amanda

"Alright nigga, you ain't just going fuck me and feed me room service. What we doing today?" I asked Harlem who had a look of satisfaction on his face. He better be satisfied, we had been confined to this room, sucking and fucking since Ashleigh left five days ago. She called Houston's phone from Harlem's phone so I knew she was good and it sounded like they were having fun.

"Shit I ain't going fuck you *and* feed you room service. I'm only fucking you, that room service getting charged to your room. That's your bill when you check out." He said falling out like shit was funny. Over the past couple of days, I have come to realize that his ass had more jokes then all of the kings of comedy all put together. He would crack jokes on me and I would crack them right the fuck back.

"It's cool baby, money ain't a thing and I always feed the needy." I said throwing a stack of money his way and watching it rain on his body. I watched as his eyes damn near bulged out of his head. I know his ass thought I was some broke ass female that was on the look for a come up but that wasn't me. I didn't need a nigga, I was what a nigga needed.

"Man, if you don't pick up your rent and car note." He joked again as I made my way to the bathroom, making sure I put on a show with the way my lips were swinging.

"Baby both of my vehicles are paid for and I'm far from a teen. We don't pay rent around these parts, I pay a mortgage cause issa home owner." I said blowing him a kiss before heading in the bathroom for a shower. Passing by the mirror I shook my head at my reflection. My hair was a mess and there were passion marks covering my chest and neck. Turning to the side I observed more on my ass plus what appeared to be this nigga's hand print. I couldn't do anything but laugh because I wasn't complaining when the shit happened so why start now, right? Jumping in the shower I ran through my head what I wanted to wear for the day but that was short lived. Thoughts of Houston found their way to the forefront of my brain.

Initially, I wanted to say I was taking one for the team by staying with him for the week. I wanted to say I was only here with him so that Ashleigh wouldn't think I was lonely and cute her escapade short. The honest to God truth was, I was enjoying this man's company. He made me feeling things I hadn't felt in forever. Things I hadn't felt since... Mannie. It wasn't love, couldn't be love this early in the game. If I am still being honest, I don't know what this was but I know I was happy. I know that I hadn't cried myself to sleep since I've been in his presence. I know that I've never had the urge to be in a nigga's face since Mannie, yet here I was not wanting to part with this man. And I could see he didn't want to leave my side either. From day one, his phone constantly rang and outside of calls from his brother and cousin it went unanswered. The same could be said for mine. I knew there were bitches calling him just like he knew niggas were calling me, that just didn't matter to us.

"Damn, I know I dirtied that pussy but get yo ass out of there I gotta piss." He ignorant ass called out as he banged on the bathroom door.

"Go pee in the lobby nigga." I shouted back. I felt the breeze as he opened the door, dick just swinging from side to side hitting his thighs, and lifted the toilet seat. "Houston what the fuck are you doing?" I asked. I mean I knew what he was doing but I enjoyed my privacy and he was invading that. After living by yourself for years your private time is sacred to you.

"About to piss. You was in here playing like a nigga was going to hold that shit for you. And stop watching me unless you goin come hold the motherfucker." He said causing me to roll my eyes.

"Alright." I said cutting off the water and stepping out.

"Alright what?" he laughed as he turned to the toilet and started to use the bathroom like I wasn't here.

"Nah you told me to hold it so I'm going fucking hold it." I said stepping forward like I was really going to grab it. The arrogant motherfucker wasn't even holding it, just standing there with his legs spread and hands at his side.

"Man, back yo retarded ass up." He said laughing, "Hit yo ass with the dick and now you want to hold it through whatever." He finished shaking his dick off and reaching behind me to start the shower for himself. "Aye dress casual, I'm taking yo ass do something to that mess on your head." He called out stepping in the shower.

"Nigga you crazy if you think one of your bitches going do something to my fucking hair." I spat.

"Aye, watch your mouth. Only I can call my bitches, bitches. You call them team mates ma. Anyway, my cousin Toya going hook yo shit up. Ashleigh on her way up there now, twin must have fucked up her shit too." He laughed as I walked out the bathroom and over to the closet where my clothes were. Knowing Houston ass, he was taking me to the hood so I knew to leave the heels alone. Now don't think I'm downing the hood cause I'm not. I came from the hood and was damn near raised by the hood so it was love there. I just couldn't live there anymore because the hood took my parents, so its hate there too. Selecting my outfit took no time and I grabbed a pair of tennis and accessories. I slid into a red lace bra and boy short set before sitting down in front of the mirror and pulling my hair back into a high bun and slicking my baby hair down.

"Damn you make red look good." Houston said walking out of the bathroom leaving a trail of water behind him. Nigga just said fuck drying off I guess.

Opting out of rocking any make up, I slid on the white ripped up jean shorts, burgundy crop top and a pair of Heiress 11's. I slid some gold hoops in my ear and gold bangles around my wrist before giving myself a nod of approval. I laughed when I noticed Houston throw on some black basketball shorts and a burgundy tea with some Nike slides. This nigga was so hood.

"What's funny?" He asked.

"You are so hood Houston. Why your ass threw on basketball shorts knowing we are going somewhere today?" I asked.

"Shit we ain't going nowhere important. Who I'm trying to impress ma?" he asked grabbing his cell phone and a knot of money. I shook my head and grabbed my shades and chap stick as I followed him out the room. It didn't take valet long to bring his Audi around and we were sliding in the soft seats. I know I had a nice ass Audi but this one was bossy as the fuck.

"Aye sit yo ass back and calm down. Touching on all my shit like you ten." He snapped as I played with all the features of his car. I stopped for a moment until his phone rung and he was preoccupied with his conversation. Opening the middle console, I nosily went through his belongings until he snapped it closed barely missing my hand.

"I would have kicked your ass if that caught me." I mouthed with my finger in his face since he was still on the phone. Pulling out my phone I went through Instagram liking shit to occupy my time while he talked on the phone. What I really wanted to do was eavesdrop on his conversation but it was one sided and he was simply listening. Midway through my stalking of Ming Lee's page he finally spoke.

"Maaaaan, you sure Kwame can't handle that shit? I'm busy right now." He said running his hand over his face. There was a pause in which he looked my way, shrugged his shoulders then answered. "Nigga I'm coming and I'm trying to be in and out so have that ready for me." He said before hanging up the phone. I could tell he was going deal with something illegal and either didn't want me to know where his stash was or didn't want me to get caught in a crossfire. Anyway, it goes he was good bringing me around. Loyalty was instilled in me since the day I met Mannie and nothing would change on my part.

"You can bring me back to the room if you need to. I can call a uber, all I need is the address to the shop." I suggested. He looked at me for a second too long before answering.

"Nah you straight. I gotta make a detour then we can go do something to that nappy ass head." He said mushing me.

"NAPPY?" I asked loudly. "Nigga find a nap in this head and I'll give you a stack." I challenged.

"A stack per nap? Shit I'm about to be Oprah rich." He laughed as I smacked him behind the head. "Aye keep your hands to yourself." He laughed again. "What you mixed with?"

"Nigga." I answered.

"Your hair tells a different story." He said insulting me. I hate when niggas act like foreign bitches the only ones that can have nice hair. Black women don't have to be mutts to have desirable hair.

"What kind of childish ass question is that? Nigga I can't just be black with nice hair?" I spat. "You just pissed me the fuck off. Shut up talking to me."

"Damn my bad ma. That was a fuck up on my part but you ain't gotta be so fucking serious. Calm your ass down. I just assumed you were mixed because of the texture." He explained.

"Well I'm full blown black, meaning not mixed with shit." I put an end to the petty argument. After a moment of silence, I came clean. "The bitch this hair came from ain't a nigga though." I said before falling out laughing. I made this whole argument knowing this was a full lace wig, courtesy of some bald bitch in Malaysia. "Let em find out I had you feeling bad." I said pinching his cheek.

"Nah I was about to drop yo ass off in the middle of the hood and shoot the fuck out." He laughed pulling up into the yard of a nice house. The neighborhood wasn't the best but it wasn't the worst either. I opened the door and went to get out but before one of my Jordan's could touch the ground I was pulled back into the car. "Nah you stay yo ass in the car. Lock the doors and don't unlock them bitches for nobody. I'll be right out." He said making me roll my eyes but close the door like he said. I watched as he reached in the middle console

and grabbed one of the guns I had seen earlier. His cocky ass
didn't even tuck it in his waistband. He just held the bitch in
his hands like it was a bag of groceries. I was too done with
him when he waved at the old ass neighbor with the gun in
his hand. The old man hauled ass into the house. For
someone who said he would be in and out, 10 minutes later I
was still waiting on his ass. Pulling my eyes away from my
kindle app where I was reading Gangsta's Paradise by Latoya
Nicole, my heart started beating double time.

"Oh, baby fuck no." I said opening the console and
grabbing the remaining gun. The bitch didn't even have
bullets in it but only Houston and I knew that shit. I don't
know what kind of gun it was but I figured if you shot one
you shot them all, right? Opening the door, I lightly closed it
then dropped low around the side of the car. Houston wanted
to take all fucking long in the house and look what the fuck
was going on. I made a dash to the other side of the house
and tip toed my ass up the back. Crouching back down I
slowly made my way to the side of the house until I was
directly behind my victim. Standing to my feet I grabbed a
handful of dreads and smirked as I placed the cold steel to the
side of his head.

"What the..." he started before I tightened my grip on his
hair, snatched his head back and spoke.

"Shut the fuck up! Nigga make one fucking noise and
today will easily turn into the worst day of your life.
Somebody else in that house?" I asked. "All I need is a nod or

a shake of the head." When he shook his head no I knocked him across his shit with the back of the gun. His head immediately started bleeding. "I don't like being lied to but it's cool, we going in there together. Walk!" I demanded still clutching the gun and his dreads. Walking in the house I noticed it was beautifully decorated. Almost like and older couple would live here with their family. Checking the bottom portion and concluding it was empty, we made our way upstairs. There were no walls in this portion. Just one big open ass floor. The tables in the room were bare with the exception of one which is where Houston was. Upon hearing us walk in he held his gun up and trained it on us. On impulse, I snatched the gun from the dude's waistband in front of me and pushed him forward as I trained my guns on each of them.

"Bitch you set me up?" Houston spat with hate in his eyes. I was confused for a second until I realized what it looked like.

"Nigga no." I removed the gun from his direction and pointed them both to ole dude. "I caught his ass trying to come in the window and stopped his ass." I explained. What I didn't expect was for him to fall out laughing.

"Man, you wild." He said. "Jury, you let this lil bitty ass woman hem you up with an empty gun?" He asked falling out laughing. I mugged him as Jury mugged me. "Nigga wait until everybody hear about this shit."

"Bitch that gun was empty?" He spat walking towards me.

75

"That one was but yours ain't. Take another step and I'll make good on that promise." I said with a smirk. "Besides, if he wouldn't have said anything you wouldn't have known the difference."

"Where the fuck you found this bitch at? Her ass seriously wanna lay me out!" Jury asked Houston who was staring at me. I couldn't place the look in his eyes. His stare was making me uncomfortable though.

"Why the fuck was you coming in the window nigga?" I asked.

"The shit was jammed so I was trying to open it from outside. I should fuck you up for hitting me with that gun." He said removing his shirt and holding it to his head.

"Oh, my bad." I shrugged. "I would love to give you back your shit but you still look mad, I think I'll hold on to it." I told him lowering the gun. Looking up Houston was still staring my way and it was freaking me out. "I'm going to the car. Houston, my hair!" I reminded him as I walked out. The look in his eyes was familiar but I didn't need him falling in love with a bitch. I wasn't looking for love, that wasn't in the plans. I just wanted a stiff dick and a death stroke. Nothing more, nothing less.

Chapter 9

Houston

"Nigga you straight?" Jury asked as soon as Amanda walked out the room.

"Nigga hell nah I ain't ok. Did you just see that shit? Shorty just fucked my head up." I admitted while grabbing the last bag of money from the loose floor board. I was supposed to be in and out of this bitch but Jury had some shit with him. I couldn't be mad at the nigga cause he didn't like all this extra shit. He didn't handle drugs or money. His only job was killing niggas, thus his name. He and his brother, Judge, were certified crazy ass niggas. They didn't believe in a kill getting away. They really believed they were the judge and the jury, therefore your life was in their hands. To see his big ass, get handled by Amanda lil ass had me side eyeing him. While I was side eyeing him, I was fascinated by her.

"Aye I got a question. You feeling that chick?" Jury asked pulling me from my thoughts while stroking his chin.

"Nah I'm just fucking her." I lied because what I was feeling had nothing to do with my dick. I wasn't ready to admit that shit aloud yet though.

"Good." He said and started to walk out.

"The fuck you mean good?" I asked wondering where the fuck he was going with this. "What that have to do with you?"

"I'm killing her. Her ass really went across my shit" He stated like he just said he was hungry or some shit like that. This why I couldn't be around that nigga too often. Him and Judge felt like murder was as easy as flicking a light off. I guess to them it was.

"Woah my nigga, no you ain't." I said mugging him.

"Why not? If you only fucking her, you ain't got a shortage of pussy." He said putting me on front street.

"Nigga she just saved my life!" I said.

"From who? Me? Nigga she ain't do shit but piss me off! Your life wasn't in danger so how she saved it? Your ass ain't just fucking her, you in love." He said nodding his head. "I could see that and she saw it from how you were staring at her. You know that's why she hauled ass out of here right?" He said telling me what the fuck I already knew.

"Man, she ain't like the other bitches." I came clean. "She ain't fucking with me cause I'm Houston. She doesn't give a fuck about Houston. How many bitches you know was going come to my rescue like that? She ain't know that you were my nigga but she didn't give a fuck. Nigga she grabbed an empty hammer and still wasn't spooked by you. Told you she would end your shit with a smile. She different. When I say go left her sassy ass goes right unless it's some serious shit. I'm used to yes bitches and that shit gets boring after a while. A nigga can fuck with a challenge and that's what she is. You know me though Jury, I ain't never wanted one woman. Monogamy scares the fuck out of a nigga." I confessed as he nodded.

"Maybe your ass just ain't ran into a woman that made you want to be with just her. You got these cookie cutter bitches on your dick and they all the same to you. Why stick with one if the next one is just like the last. Ain't no different so you get comfortable with all them bitches. When you meet a woman that's different from the normal, that shit makes you want to come home to her. You never know what the fuck to expect. She gives you a vibe you can't find with the rest of these bitches so you stop looking. Take Lika for example, I used to dog her like I dogged any female I was fucking. A nigga didn't know how to breathe when she started doing me dirty. I thought I had her dickmitazed and she was waiting by the phone for me to call. One day I was checking into a hotel with a shorty and she was with some nigga checking in. She didn't scream or flash out on me. In fact, she smiled, dapped me up and went about her business. I decided in that moment she was enough. Well I mean after I killed that nigga in front of her, I decided she was enough." He laughed as he relived that memory. Only person I know that's crazier than Jury is his wife, Malika. They deserved each other.

"Shit Malika wanted yo ass though. Amanda don't want me, she just wants my dick. She made it clear that she wasn't looking for love, a relationship or nothing equivalent to it." I confessed.

"Show me a woman that ain't looking for love and I'll show you a woman that has been hurt. Find out what broke her heart and fix that shit. Then it's yours." He said standing to his feet.

"I tried to ask why she was so closed off. Her ass shut me down then took the dick." I said as he fell out laughing.

"Take her to Bella!" As soon as he said that I knew I would be getting my answers.

****

"This don't look like no damn restaurant or salon Houston!" Amanda snapped as soon as I pulled into the driveway. Her ass slept for the hour and a half it took to get here and the first thing she does is run off at the mouth.

"Shit Bella cooks and lays edges, you sleep." I told her as I hopped out the car. I didn't even wait for her as I climbed the staircase up to the door.

"Who the fuck is Bella?" She asked as the door came swinging open.

"I'm Bella and Houston why you bringing bitches to my house announced?" She said as Amanda looked behind her then got down to look under the car.

"You need help finding something?" I asked thinking she dropped an earring or something. At this point it was daylight but she turned the flashlight on her phone and was still looking under the car.

"Nah, I don't need help. Nothing under here." She said standing to her feet.

"What you looking for?" I asked

"The bitches Bella think you brought up here. She better go the fuck back in the house before I have her ass on this ground reaching for a life alert. She don't know me and I promise she don't want too. Yo dumb ass come bring me way to Timbuctoo for me to go straight to hell for beating up on the fucking elderly." She spat as my mouth dropped in shock. I was a disrespectful ass nigga but I met my match in this firecracker.

"I'm about to give this hoe the beating she never knew she needed." Bella said walking up on Amanda who stepped forward too. Placing my body in between them I couldn't believe shit had went left. I almost wanted to laugh but Amanda was disrespectful as the fuck.

"Who ass you goin beat maw?" Amanda asked. If she really wanted to, they could both touch each other because they were damn near standing face to face. I was positioned to where I could stop the though. I had never seen anyone so much as talk back to Bella so this I kind of wanted to see.

"You new age hoes need to learn manners. Who the fuck raised you?" She spat.

"The streets!" Amanda spat back before she blew in Bella's face.

"Bitch did you just blow in my face?" Bella asked looking shocked.

"Where I'm from spitting in someone's face is mad disrespectful and I'm not THAT disrespectful so I did the next best. I don't care how old you are, you ain't about to play with me." Amanda said rolling her eyes. "Who the fuck are you anyway?" She asked.

"Who the fuck is halfway disrespectful?" She asked laughing making Amanda join in. "You lucky I can't fight and I'm all mouth. I would fuck you up. I'm his mama by the way." She said before turning around and going to the door. "Bring y'all ugly asses in and take ya fucking shoes off at the door." She called over her shoulder.

"Bruh you just treated my moms like she was someone off of the streets." I said looking at her in amazement.

"And I ain't apologizing so you and her can get that out ya'll mind. Mama or not her ass tried me. She better have some food cooked too cause I'm hungry. Remind me when I leave here to fuck you up! I don't meet families and I fight mother in laws." She said pushing past me and into the house. Fuck what she said, she said she don't do mother in laws. Was she opening up to the idea of us?

Walking into the house, I bypassed the kitchen where the women were still bickering and went to the office that Harlem and I kept here. Pressing my thumb into the pad, I waited as it read my fingerprint and listened for the click. Pushing my way into the office I made sure it was closed behind me before heading to the safe and placing the money safely inside. I wanted to give them a moment to talk so I hit Harlem's line.

"Hello." Came a feminine voice. I knew it was Brooklyn because he hadn't been letting shorty out of his sight. That's didn't stop me from picking on her though.

"Felicia what are you doing answering bro phone?" I asked stifling my laughter.

"I'm not Felicia, but he asked me to answer. Harlem, I can hear your ignorant ass laughing. Don't get you and Felicia beat up." She laughed before my brother's voice filled the line.

"Stop playing with my lil mama nigga." He laughed.

"Shit, she wasn't fun anyway. I expected her to flash out or something. Amanda would have cursed yo ass out for calling her another chick's name." I said laughing.

"Her and Amanda situation ain't the fucking same." He mumbled. I heard something in his voice but didn't know what the tone was.

"You need to speak on something?" I asked. I heard ruffling and movement on his end so I figured he went into another room. As I waited for him to get situated I shot my mama a text message.

"Man, Brooklyn can't get pissed off about you mentioning a bitch name because she got a whole nigga home." He shocked me. She didn't seem like the cheating type and he wasn't the boyfriend number two type.

"She on some snake shit? How you found out?" I questioned.

"Nah she ain't being snake. That nigga ain't shit. He put his hands on her and the nigga a drunk. She damn near taking care of him. That ain't her man, he her son." He said sounding frustrated.

"Shit no matter what way you flip this shit, shorty is taken. Don't get your feelings involved on some temporary shit." I said like I wasn't involved in some temporary shit.

"It might be too late for that. Let me hit you back. I'm taking shorty shopping and get her a phone, she lost her jack in the club the night we met them. I want to wine and dine her, you know they only have a couple days left here." He reminded me and there was a tightness in my chest. I didn't want Amanda to leave. As soon as the thought crossed my mind my mama texted me to come get this cry baby out of her kitchen. Ending the call, I headed to the kitchen where Amanda was in tears.

"Ma what you told her?" I questioned knowing she did just what I texted her to do. I asked her to break down that tough persona. Bella will read you from cover to cover despite how strong your facade is. Jury was right about me coming here. Without answering me, my mom walked out the kitchen and mouthed for me to talk to her.

"Shorty what's wrong? Moms beat yo ass?" I asked trying to crack a joke.

"I can't be here with you! I can't do this!" She cried out loud. I could tell this was one of those long overdue cries so I let her get it out before I asked her to elaborate.

"What you mean you can't do this? Do what?" I asked. "You goin have to talk in complete sentences ma."

"I don't want to like you. I can't fall in love with you! I love Mannie and only Mannie." She cried out making me stop stroking her hair and immediately freeze up. So, she was like Brooklyn, her ass had a nigga to.

"Ma, I ain't competing with another nigga walking this green earth. If you want me to bring you back to the room I can. Then you can hit up Mannie to come get yo ass." I said damn near spitting out his name.

"I wish I could." She cried. "God, you don't know how I wish Heaven had a phone number. Why he left me here lost and confused? For years, I held him down and in five days you've come in and changed everything. I don't wanna fall for you." She cried tugging at my heart. How do I answer that shit?

Chapter 10

Ashleigh

The past few days have been some of the most amazing days I've ever had. Nicki Minaj wasn't lying when she said, to live doesn't mean you're alive. I was finally alive and happy! Harlem made me feel alive and happy. I questioned if this all happened too fast and concluded that I deserved this. After giving my all to a fuck nigga imagine what I could give to a boss. Fuck what time or anyone had to say, I deserved this shit. Standing in the floor length mirror in the hotel room, I felt like Julia Roberts in Pretty Woman. The way the red mermaid style dress hugged my curves was jaw dropping. The dress looked made for me and me alone. The nude Jimmy Choo heels were the perfect complement to my attire and the jewelry damn near made hell freeze over. Although Today was nothing short of perfection and I had Harlem to thank for that. When he woke me up with breakfast in bed I wasn't surprised because this has been happening since day one. He spoiled me more than I had ever been spoiled in life and I was grateful. After breakfast, he got me a cell phone that I told him I didn't need. My last cell phone was in Dre's name and I would just do an insurance claim for a new one when I got back home. I would also swap the plan to my name before he got his walking papers.

Although we had been shopping more times than I could count, this time was different. Harlem left me alone with a driver and his black card with instructions. I was told to get an evening gown, accessories and shoes no matter the cost. Then the driver took me to a Salon where Toya, Harlem's cousin laid my hair. After finishing I was whisked off to a beauty bar where my makeup, nails, toes, brows and lashes were done. Sliding back into the car I was met with roses on the seat, a gift bag and a card. Inside the gift bag were some of the most expensive pieces of jewelry I had ever dreamed of. The earrings, bracelet and necklace were dripping with diamonds and I made the executive decision that it would replace what I picked out to go with my gown. The card simply told me, he would see me in the lobby at 8. I decided in that moment, I was ready for him. He was so understanding when I told him I didn't want to be sexually active with him just yet and my mind was changed. Not because of the jewelry and the clothing. No, my mind was changed because this incredible man was like nothing or no one that I would come into contact with again. I wanted him in the worst way so today I would make that happen. Asking the driver to make one more stop I planned my night in my head. This would be more magical than Disney world to a kid. After getting myself ready, I made my way to the lobby with minutes to spare and he was there looking like a snack. The night was nothing short of perfection. The dinner was romantic and so was the carriage ride through the park but I couldn't focus on that. My focus was on this very moment.

Standing in front of the mirror I snapped a picture of myself and sent it to Amanda before I slide the silk like material off of my body and let it fall at my feet. Lifting it from the ground, I quickly made my way to the rest room and freshened myself up. Knowing I was pressed for time and he would be back with the wine I lied and said I needed, I slipped on a red sheer bra and thong set with a pair of Red peep toe Louboutin's. I decided not to take off the jewelry. I wasn't a pro at the sexy thing but I think I was doable. The room was already set up so I ran around to light the candles that were placed around in various places. Setting the tone was easy because I already planned on putting Seems like you're ready on repeat. If my appearance didn't prove that, the song would let him know that I was indeed ready. Climbing into the bed, I propped myself in the middle of the bed so that I was facing the door. Nerves set in like this was my very first time. I toyed with what position I would lie in until I settled on laying on my side with my legs extended and my hand holding my head up creating this sexy cascading effect with my hair. My heart began beating double time when I heard the key card being slide into the door. Any second now he would turn the corner and see me and I didn't know what his reaction would be.

"Aye Brooklyn, why the fuck all the lights off?" He called out and I had to stop myself from laughing. I was going for sexy and this nigga flicked the lights on.

"Really Harlem!" I called out as he looked up from his phone and took in the scene before him. The phone and the bottle of wine hit the floor and he wasn't the least bit concerned. I watched as his eyes roamed the length of my body. Initially, I thought I saw hunger in his eyes but after ten seconds of him saying nothing I became self-conscious and attempted to cover up.

"Nah ma don't do that. Don't cover up, please don't cover up." He said walking over and removing my hands from my body. "Damn, you should never cover up." He said bringing his lips to meet mine. The kiss we shared was the sweetest most passionate kiss ever. I felt his want for me in that single kiss. I felt his need for me in that single kiss. When our lips parted I heard the whimper before I could stop myself. I never wanted it to end and the pout on my face showed that. "Wait let me run this shit back. I ruined yo set up. Get back in position." He told me as he backed out the room after turning the lights back off. Why did my ass really lay back down like I was a second ago? I heard the key card once again and felt my pussy react to what I was sure would be a night to remember. The fact that he was replaying this moment for real, made the nerves subside. I couldn't help the laughter that left my mouth when he walked back in butt ass naked, dick leading the way.

"Really Harlem?" I laughed aloud.

"Shhhh, you goin fuck up the mood." He was dead ass serious walking towards the bed. The list was evident in his eyes. Just the look he was giving me made me moan out and he hadn't even laid a finger on me. Within seconds he closed the distance between us and my thighs burned from his touch.

"Harlem." I moaned out as he crawled onto the bed and his lips pressed into my neck. The slow sensual kisses he placed along my collar bone made me shiver in anticipation for what was to come.

"I like this shit." He said fingering the bra I was wearing. Before I could utter a thank you or anything he grabbed the bra in between both of his hands and ripped it as if it was paper. My mouth dropped open in shock but his formed into a sexy smirk at the sight of my breast bouncing freely. "It looked nice on you but that shit looks way better off." He said before attacking my breast like they were filled with milk and he was a starving infant. I felt his hands near my center before feeling the panties ripped off of my ass. I wanted to argue about how much I loved that set but the feeling of Harlem's fingers slipping and sliding into my pussy put me into another mind frame. It's like my pussy was a piano and he had mastered every key to the perfect song. If this man was performing this magic with his fingers what would he do with his dick?

"Hmmmm Harlem. Fuck!" I called out surprising myself. I had never been vocal during sex but this man was bringing out another side of me. I felt his lips and tongue tracing a pathway to where his fingers had made a home. I felt his warm breath before I was passionately paralyzed as his tongue replaced his fingers. The memory of days ago when he took me on a roller coaster with this very mouth flooded my mind. "Mmmmm..." I moaned out as I attempted to twist out of his grasp. I needed a moment. To think or to understand, just to escape this moment. The intensity would send me to an early grave if he didn't let me catch my mind.

"Stop fucking running." He growled into my pussy. The vibration of his words mixed with the motion of his tongue drove me over the limit of control, within seconds I was trying to remove his head from between my thighs.

"Wait, Harlem I need the bathroom." I panicked. The urge to jump up and run to the restroom was strong but his grip was stronger.

"Ma, I fucking love you!" He moaned out. "I swear I fucking love you!" He repeated.

"I love you too." I moaned without a second thought. This felt too right. There was the tingling in my chest again before I erupted and flowed over like a volcano. If I would have died in this very moment, the past few minutes made it all worthwhile. This man had to be God because in this moment I was at the highest of the high. Or so I thought. Just when I thought I couldn't get higher, he took me to our personal Heaven. His dick snaked through my pussy like it was created just for me. The high I was getting from him sliding in and out of me would have me looking for him in the daytime with a flashlight. "Harlem, fuck me." I cried into his ear as he made love to me like I would break. That's not what I needed right now, I wanted his dick to tap dance on my uterus. The mischievous smirk he gave me let me know that I was in for something serious.

"You sure about that ma?" He asked licking his lips. Grabbing my hips, he lifted them from the bed and shoved his dick into my pussy causing my juices to squirt out. "That's what the fuck you wanted?" He asked pounding into my pussy. The noises that we were making was turning me on. My pussy had never been so wet.

"Yes! Yes! Harlem just like that!" I screamed out leaving scratches down his back.

"Turn that ass over!" He demanded turning me onto my stomach where I immediately assumed the perfect arch. He had no idea the level of freak that this position brought out of me. I felt his dick at my entrance as he played in my juices and took him by surprise when I slammed my ass down, instantly taking him all in. "Goddamn" he groaned grabbing my waist and holding them so that he could gain control of the situation. The thought was nice but I had plans for him. Placing my feet on the floor I decided to tease him and made my ass clap on his dick. Looking back, I smirked as I noticed his eyes rolling to the back of his head before they connected with mine. "Oh, that shit funny?" He asked before applying pressure to my waist and fucking the lining out of my pussy. This time when I came, he followed. Falling flat onto the with him inside of me I caught my breath thinking this was it until later. Wrong! I felt his dick growing inside of me and the moisture in my pussy welcomed it.

Chapter 11

Amanda

The tears wouldn't stop falling as I softly closed the door to the room and took the last of my luggage to the front desk. With every step, I took to the elevator it felt like my feet got heavier and heavier. The closer I got, the harder it was for me to move forward with my decision. Something told me with Houston is where I needed to be and that scared me. I found myself forgetting about Mannie while in his presence. An hour ago, I attempted to remember his scent and it pained me when I realized I couldn't I was intoxicated by Houston's scent and as good as he smelled. In the moment, I felt like I needed to smell Mannie. My home still held his smell so that's where I was headed, to be near Mannie. I needed to be near him so bad that I booked a flight straight in to Lafayette, leaving my car in New Orleans. I would worry about that later; a rental was already waiting at the airport to get me home.

"You can load these in the car. Tell him give me one more moment and I'll be ready to go." I told the attendant as I handed him the room key card and made my way back towards the elevator that carried me to Harlem and Ashleigh's room. Leaving my friend behind wasn't in the plans but neither was betraying Mannie. I mean yes, I've fucked other niggas since he's died and not felt anything. Not regret or whatever the fuck I was feeling now. The problem was the tears that are falling, aren't tears of regret for the past few days. I don't regret meeting Houston, fucking him or opening up to him. I regret the decision that I'm making now. I regret that I'm sneaking out of the hotel after expressing my feelings for him and him for me. I'm regretting that I told him I would be here and as soon as he opens his eyes in the morning he will see that I am a liar. I won't be there. I can't be there for him the way he needs me to. I'm not available, I'm taken by the greatest man to walk this earth. I would forever be taken. Getting to the room I prayed that it was Ashleigh that answered and not Harlem. I didn't need him interfering in my escape. Tapping on the door quickly I waited as I heard shuffling around. I thought about the flight that I would be catching in the next couple of hours and the tears fell again as the door slowly opened and Ashleigh stepped out.

"What's going on?" She asked with sleep in her eyes. I saw the passion marks all over her body since the robe she had on left hardly anything to the imagination. The glow she sported let me know my friend had finally gotten some but I couldn't dwell on that. "What did he do to you!" She asked with more bass in her voice noticing the tears.

"Shhhh, you will wake Harlem. He didn't do anything that I didn't need." I responded.

"What the fuck does that mean?" She asked looking furious causing me to realize I sounded like a battered woman that accepted the beatings.

"He made me love him Ashleigh. And I- I can't do that." I cried. "Mannie doesn't deserve that." I said falling into her open arms. For moments, she just stroked my hair and let me get the tears out. Even when a group of women passed by with their heels in their hand she never spoke a word. She was just there as I let my tears soak her robe. Getting myself together I told her the reason I was even bothering her. "Umm..." I started.

"What's wrong?" She asked searching my eyes for an answer.

"Listen, I don't want you to leave. You are having fun and I want that to continue. Spend the rest of your week here and of course I'll have your ticket ready and I'll pick you up from the airport. I can't stay here, I'm leaving." The words spilled from my mouth in one breath. I saw sadness fill her eyes and knew what she was about to say before she said it. I immediately shook my head. "No, you stay!"

"Amanda, if you're leaving so am I." She said in a firm tone. "Harlem will understand." She explained with a forced smile.

"That's the thing Ash, I'm leaving and not telling Houston. I don't want Houston to get wind of me leaving or he will ask me to stay. And if he asks I won't leave."

"Then why don't you just stay?" She asked sounding frustrated.

"I can't." My voice broke as a fresh set of tears fell from my eyes.

"Ok, I'll meet you downstairs in a few minutes. Most of my things are already packed so you can send someone up to help me." She said before turning to walk back into her room. The way her shoulders dropped and I saw the water in her eyes made me feel terrible. I didn't want her to leave because I liked Harlem for her but her mind was set. After taking the elevator down and stopping to let them know she needed help with bags I slide into the awaiting car. Immediately my mind replayed the reason behind my departure and the tears began again.

"Well, I snuck out the room like I was a hoe that stole his money while he was asleep." Ashleigh said pulling me from my thoughts as she slid into the car with tears falling down her face. Digging into my purse I handed her the cell phone she thought was missing. I snatched it from the bar the night we met the guys. I knew if I had not done that she would have never had the fun she had. She would be too worried about Dre and the many threats he was throwing her way and I couldn't have that.

"I'm sorry you had to leave him." Was all I could offer.

"It's okay, I'll see him again. I have to get rid of my houseguest and then I can focus on Harlem and if we have a future. I just hopes he understands why I left him with no goodbyes." She said shocking me, I had never heard her sound so adamant about leaving Dre. In fact, I had never heard her say she was leaving him before and I was happy that the decision was made. "Oh, and you can have that phone because it is in Dre's name, I don't want anything to do with him. As a matter of fact…" she said rolling down the window and throwing it out onto the street. "…fuck Dre." She said making me clap my hands.

"Yaaaasssss best friend." I cheered her on before we settled into a comfortable silence. I'm not sure what hers was full of but mine was split between two men, Houston and Mannie. The four-hour flight was quick and by the time we landed Ashleigh's mood matched mine.

"Back to reality." She mumbled shrugging. I felt horrible, I was the reason she had to prematurely run back to Dre.

"Do you want to stay to my house for the next couple of days. Hell, you can move in forever." I offered for the millionth time.

"No, I have to get this over with. I know you want to get home so I ordered an uber when we landed." She told me as we grabbed our luggage.

"What? I would drop you home." I said massaging my head to ease some of the throbbing I felt from the headache that came from nowhere.

"I know you would have. I'm fine Amanda, I'm grown." She replied hugging me before we parted ways. I watched her until she disappeared out of the doors and fought myself on making her come home with me. The truth was I needed to be alone with my thoughts, so I let her go. After getting the rental, I had no choice but to make a stop at Walgreens because I was out of Aspirin and this headache wouldn't quit. Walking through the aisles. I grabbed the medicine, snacks and drinks before I remembered that Houston and I hadn't use condoms last night. A baby wasn't in the plans so my feet carried me to the pharmacy for a plan B.

"Amanda?" I heard behind me and my body stiffened. I would never forget that voice for as long as I lived. Knowing that I didn't want to nut up in front of all of these innocent bystanders, I deserted my basket and left the store. There were other Walgreens in Lafayette, one of them would have to do. As I unlocked the car door, I heard the sound of heels behind me and spun around.

"I'm telling you right now, I'm not the same Amanda you knew. I will whip your ass all up and down this parking lot if you open your mouth to disrespect me." I snapped as I stood face to face with Pamela Powers, Mannie's mother. She looked different but I will never forget the way that woman treated me like I wasn't shit when Mannie died. I still cried because I could not attend his funeral and say my final goodbyes. She knew more than anyone, what he meant to me and me to him but she didn't care.

"I'm not here to argue with you Amanda. I just wanted to..." She said with her hands up in surrender. I hated that she saw me here like this. I always said when his family laid eyes on me again, they would see that I was still living the way he told me I should be. Like the boss lady he told me I was. They were supposed to see me dripped in ice with the finest clothing yet her I was in a pink sweat suit and my hair pulled into a bun.

"Calling my name was enough to start a fucking argument and you knew that. What could you possibly want with me Pam. If I could remember the last words you spoke to me was, I was just your son's whore and a parentless gutter rat. So what could you want to tell me now?" I spat feeling all of those emotions return. For years I pushed that to the back of my brain but seeing her here was taking me back to that day.

"I just wanted to apologize about how I treated you. You didn't deserve that from me or anyone else. I know my son loved you I was just hurting…" she started before I exploded.

"YOU WERE HURTING? YOU WERE HURTING? YOU WEREN'T EVEN A REAL MOTHER TO HIM AND YOU WANT TO TELL ME YOU WERE HURTING?" I screamed through tears. "Bitch how fucking dare you sit here and speak to me about hurt. Fuck you and your feelings bitch. I hate you and can't wait until it's your time to go so I can spit on your fucking grave. You have big balls stepping to me like I'm not aware of the role you played in his life. Let me remind you of my position, I was his every fucking thing! In life and in death it will forever be Mannie and Manda, bitch! We didn't have secrets, that nigga knew when I shit and how many fucking times I wiped. So, I knew all about the type of mother you were. He wanted to go to school, he told me that. I know that when he graduated high school you were the one that guilt trip him to stay in the streets. He wanted out and you made him feel like it was his responsibility to make sure you had a home and money. The streets took him out because you kept him in them!" I finished as she nodded her head.

"Mannie, was in the streets because he knew that was quick money. That had nothing to do with me." She lied through her gap ass teeth.

"Lie to someone that didn't know, not me." I countered.

"You didn't have a problem spending all of that money, so don't complain about it now. I saw you in the fancy whips and nice clothes just like I was."

"But which one of us deserved tat shit, Pam? Which one of us was in the traps with Mannie? Which one of us was catching plays with him, huh? Which one of us was shoving that shit up our pussies when the cops got behind us, Pam? Huh, I can't hear yo ass now. I earned my keep, did you? Let me tell you something, that money didn't make or break me. If he had a regular nine to five, I would be perfectly fine with that. I slept on the floors of some of the nastiest places before, downgrading wouldn't have done anything to me." I spat.

"Amanda, listen…" she started again.

"Nah, you listen. We ain't goin replay this shit here. If you see me somewhere else, bitch go blind. If you think of speaking my name, bite your motherfucking tongue. Stay away from me Pam because next time I will happily break yo old ass down like a fraction." I finished hoping in my car and slamming the door. I was so pissed off I was shaking as I pulled off. I heard her screaming something but I left her and that lopsided wig sitting in the parking lot. My fucking head hurt even more than it did when I got here.

Chapter 12

Ashleigh

I was glad that we flew into Lafayette because I wasn't sure I could stand the drive from New Orleans without breaking down. My body was standing in front of my house but my heart was in a room in New York. Taking a deep breath, I thanked God that it was still early in the morning and Dre would be asleep. I could deal with him later in the morning because he couldn't have any of my time at this very moment. My mind was occupied with thoughts of Harlem at the moment knowing he would wake up to an empty bed and thousands of questions yet he would get no answers. My body still remembered his touch and every time I inhaled I smelled him on me. Inhaling his scent once more I pulled out my phone and dialed his number as I quietly unlocked the front door. I know I told Amanda I would forget about him until I got rid of my houseguest but I couldn't. I was like Jazmine Sullivan in that song let it burn, call me crazy but I think I found the love of my life. As the voicemail picked up and I made it into my room I began the message that I rehearsed in my mind over and over.

"Harlem, I'm sorry I had to leave. I know that apology is shitty and you deserve so much more but that is all I can offer for now. Amanda needed me and I need you to understand that I had to be there for my girl. This week was as close to perfect as it could get. You made me feel something that I have never felt and for that I owe you. I actually just walked in the house so I have to deal with Dre. I will call you once I am a single woman because I'm coming back to you." I said before ending the message. I smiled knowing that us being apart was only for a moment. Throwing my luggage in the closet I undressed then hopped in the bed. My body was tired but in my mind, I rehearsed over and over what I would tell Dre when he woke up I know that it would not be easy to get rid of him but for Harlem and my peace of mind it would be worth it. I fell asleep with a smile on my face and woke up hours later with tears on my face.

"Ahhhhhhh Dre, what are you doing?" I screamed trying to pry his fingers from my hair. I felt my hair ripping from my scalp as he dragged me out of bed and around the room. Beyond the fire I saw dancing, I saw the gloss in his eyes and couldn't believe he was already drunk.

"You just leave with no warning bitch!" he screamed as he flung me around the room. He slurred his words and almost tripped over his own feet, releasing my hair. I took the opportunity and crawled out of the room into the hallway. If I could just reach the door, I would be fine. Before I could even make it to the living room pain shot through my body as he stomped his foot down in the middle of my back. Falling to the ground I balled into the fetal position and prayed for the beating to quickly end.

"Dre please!" I begged hoping a miracle would happen and he would quit. For a moment, I thought my prayers were answered when he walked away. When he returned moments later he held the red iPhone in my face. I died a million deaths when I heard the ringtone, Boo Thang, playing I had set the ring tone for Harlem and his name in my phone was *Boo Thang.*

"Who the fuck is this?" He asked snatching me by my hair again. The phone stopped ringing and started right back. "You better not say shit or I will kill you." He spat before answering the phone. "Hello?" he answered and I strained my ear to hear Harlem's voice. "You don't have to be quiet nigga. I know my bitch was up to no good for the past week but don't worry she ran back to daddy. I'm about to drop this dick in her and remind her where home is." Dre said laughing then disconnecting the call. "You were with that nigga?" He asked with his mouth inches from my face.

"No." I cried out lying.

"Then why the fuck did he just say have a good life. He didn't denying being with your hoe ass. So, you were fucking that nigga and left me here with my hand and some fucking porn?" he asked releasing my hair and letting my head fall back to the ground. I prayed it was over until I felt him grip my hair again. Dre pulled me to the living room where he sat in the chair and I was face to face with his erect dick.

"Dre…" I started to plead.

"Don't say shit bitch. I know you were fucking and sucking that nigga cause you a hoe. Suck my dick like you did his!" He spat as I shook my head no. "What the fuck you mean no!" he screamed grabbing my head with both of his hands and forcing his dick to my lips. When he realized I was not opening my mouth his left arm left my head and came down so hard on the side of my face that my ear started ringing. The slap had me dizzy and as soon as I cried out he forced his dick in my mouth. "Just like that." He said growing harder in my mouth as I gagged. Dre was roughly shoving his dick down my throat and there was nothing I could do but cry and gag while praying it ended. He was thrusting his hips and moaning like he wasn't raping me. "Oh, shit baby." He moaned stroking my hair and emptying his seed in my mouth. I quickly spit them out angering him even more. I was met with two slaps to the face before he started screaming again. "Did you spit out his nut! Get the fuck up and remove your clothes before I kill you!" he screamed.

Knowing I had no choice in the matter I slowly stood to my feet as he sat back, stroked his dick and watched me. I removed the pink hoodie I was wearing and went to remove the tank top before he grabbed my wrist with his free arm.

"Do that shit slow, and dance a lil bit." He demanded. It was only he and I in the room and still I was humiliated. Never had I been so disrespected in my life. I moved my hips from side to side as I slowly slid the joggers down my thighs.

"Turn around!" he called out yet another order. Doing as I was told, I faced the wall and stepped out of the joggers, leaving on my thong and bra set. Still moving my hips, I removed my bra and let it fall to the ground. I was glad to be facing the wall because he would flip out again if he saw the tears falling down my face. Why couldn't I have stayed with Harlem? I felt him stand and walk up behind me. His dick pressed into my ass while his arms wrapped around my body and palmed my breast. When he licked my ear, I wanted to vomit. "Remove those thongs, slowly." He said in my ear. The tears fell more rapidly because I didn't want Dre touching me but I knew what was coming next.

In hopes of me not being dry causing it to be painful I imagined Harlem. I imagined the way he touched me, kissed me and fucked me. When I bent down to step out of the thongs I imagined it was Harlem's arm pushing down in my back. I imagined his voice telling me to grab my ankles. When the hand slapped my ass, I imagined it was Harlem's hand too. It worked because when I was penetrated even I felt the juices drip down my thighs. Although the stroke wasn't quite right and the thickness and length was a little off, the image of Harlem caused me to moan out. I still smelled him and that thought alone cause me to cry out.

"Ooooh shit Harlem." I cried out as I came. I didn't realize my mistake until it was too late and I awaited the reaction When it didn't come I figured Dre didn't hear me because he just kept fucking me. I felt him cum with a roar before he pulled out and punched me in the back of my head causing me to fall over.

"You goin wish you didn't call me another nigga's name." he said before beating my ass like I was a nigga on the streets.

***

I don't know how I got in the bed or when did I fall asleep but looking out the window let me know the day had gone by. Climbing out of the bed was a task within itself because with every movement a different part of my body hurt. Slowly, I made my way into my bathroom and cried out from the sight of me in the mirror. I had bruises all over my face, my hair was missing in spots and my lip was busted. Seeing the redness under my left eye I knew I had to put ice on it before I would be left with a black eye. I tiptoed out of my room and bypassed Dre's room. You would think with the nut he busted before he beat my ass he would be satisfied but no, as usual he was watching porn with the volume turned to the max. Walking in the kitchen, I grabbed an ice pack from the freezer and popped a tv dinner in the microwave. I was starving and all I wanted to do was eat and go back to bed. I went back in the room where I searched for my phone then did the same in the living room with no luck. I know Dre did something with my phone and that pissed me off more than anything. I would have to ask Amanda to get Harlem's number from Houston. Walking back into the kitchen I thought my eyes were deceiving me.

"Damn girl, you look bad!" Said the naked bitch standing in my kitchen, while eating my dinner.

"I look like I'm in my motherfucking house. Who the fuck is you? And why the fuck is you naked and eating my shit" I asked getting pissed off.

"Oh, girl chill out, I'm here with Deandre. And I'm naked cause we just finished fucking. And I'm eating this pathetic dinner because of the same reason, I worked up an appetite" she laughed as she attempted to walk past me. Without thinking I grabbed her hair and pulled her to the ground. Releasing her hair, I began giving her ass just face shots. Truth is, she got the ass whipping Dre deserved. The rape, the beatings, the lies, I was releasing everything on her ass. I didn't even notice she stopped moving until I felt arms on me.

"That's enough, fuck!" I heard Dre scream before I jumped up and grabbed a knife from the counter.

"Don't fucking touch me Dre! I'm telling you right now you will never hurt me again! Pack your fucking bags because tomorrow morning, I'm going to have your ass evicted. I don't give a fuck where you go but you have to fucking go. You are a fucking burden to everyone you meet. You would want to meet up with your fucking mama and kiss ass so you can return to your couch!" I screamed finally finding my voice. This was the end of Ashleigh getting used and abused. Dre would see a different side of me.

Chapter 13

Harlem

Shit I'm a man with pride, you don't do shit like that. You don't just pick up and leave and leave me sick like that! You don't throw away what we had, just like that.

Nodding my head to the Jay-Z joint, I had to agree with his ass. This song was singing my soul and had been doing so since Brooklyn left. A bitch ain't never played me like Brooklyn did and that shit won't ever happen again. I'm not the type to get serious with a female and she had me thinking of going all the way with her. A week ago, when I woke up alone in that hotel room, I thought maybe she stepped out with Ashleigh and would be right back. When I got up to take a piss I still was clueless. It wasn't until I went to get me some clothes out of the closet that I noticed her clothes were gone. I called her phone like some lame ass stalking nigga and kept getting her voicemail. I thought something was wrong until she sent me that voicemail. After hearing the message. I still wasn't pissed off. I still blew her line up to make sure she and Ashleigh were straight. When that fuck nigga answered her phone, I wasn't pissed then either. She told me her situation at home, so how could I feel some type of way. Oh, but the moment that nigga sent me a picture of her with his dick in her mouth I saw red. She led me to believe it was nothing with them. That she was going home just to end that shit. Now, I could be wrong but when I hear someone saying they going end something I didn't know that meant to end up with a dick in their mouth.

She still consumed my thoughts for the majority of the day so I threw myself into the streets. I hadn't even been around to check on the shops because I ain't want to deal with Vontavia's whining ass. I had even been avoiding Kennedy when I knew that wasn't good for business. I was really in my feelings and feeling like, fuck bitches and get money. I think I was going through my first real heartbreak and I didn't know how to handle that shit. The only good thing out of this was it was making me a very rich man. I guess as long as the outcome is income it was well worth all of this shit I was dealing with.

"Oh, fuck no, I'm just going to drive myself." Houston said opening the car door. I was so caught up in my thoughts that I hadn't even noticed that his ass had walked out of his spot.

"Nigga, what yo ass whining about now?" I asked already knowing the answer.

"You listening to this fucking song again. You and Jay Z wasn't even going through the same thing for you to milk this song like that."

"Both of our women left us." I said shrugging.

"Nigga he was cheating and he caused his bitch to leave him. Brooklyn wasn't yours to keep and you knew that. You got your heart involved when I told you not to and now you're sitting here looking sick. Bruh you really got to shake back. You been in your feelings for a week and it has got your ass slacking." He said causing me to mug his ass. Reaching to the back seat I grabbed a bag of money and threw it on his lap.

"That's yours, I already stopped by mom and dumped a couple of these off and took my cut. Don't tell me I've been slacking when I've been doing just the opposite. Nigga I've been on my grind so don't ever question that." I spat.

"Nigga, I'm talking about in the fucking shops. That street shit ain't you so why you getting lost in it. You play the background when it comes to the streets so why the change up? I noticed your ass putting in work over there but that ain't where you need to be." He replied.

"A nigga ain't never met his daddy, don't try to be mine now. If the streets are where I want to be, then that's where I'm going to be. And another thing you never need to question is my personal situations. A nigga just going through some things. But do me a favor and don't ever act like you on a different wave then what you're on. I see that your ass is in your feelings too but you are trying hard to hide that shit. It's cool I won't speak on your situation; just know I peep your situation." I said pulling off and heading to the private dinner we were on the way to.

"Aye, fuck you." Houston replied and all I could do was laugh because he was as stubborn as my moms. He would never admit that Ashleigh had him in his feelings. All I knew was that he was left in a hotel room like I was but instead of falling into work, he was falling into every available pussy he found.

The ride was filled with wonder of why we were called over for this meeting. The product was right, the money was definitely flowing and we had no real issues in the streets that should worry Giuseppe. Initially, I wanted to decline the invitation but when a man in Giuseppe's position invites you somewhere, you go. In fact, I think him inviting us was out of respect because of the money we made him. I'm positive that even if I wanted to decline, he would make sure I was there. Houston and I were in New York flooding the streets because we had Giuseppe in our corner. Don't get it fucked up though, I always had dreams of being a made nigga so I had no problem cleaning up with or without him. My brother and I would break our wrist working to get where we needed to be, Giuseppe was just an added bonus that was appreciated.

"This nigga living large ain't he?" Houston asked as we pulled up to his estate. There was no other way to describe what laid behind the large metals gates that were heavily guarded with armed guards.

"Shit, all the money we dump in his pockets why shouldn't he be?" I asked rolling down the window as a guard approached.

"Is Mr. Moretti expecting you?" He asked.

"Nah, we just like nigga knocking and shit." Houston answered causing me to side eye his ass. This nigga was going to be the death of us. His ass is always getting us in some shit and that's my brother so I'm head first behind him, right or wrong.

"Yeah we are." I answered the guard grilling his ass back since he was grilling my twin. "Houston and Harlem Jones, why don't you get your boss on the phone and confirm that instead of grilling us." I snapped.

"Watch your mouth." He spat back clutching his gun.

"Nigga we grown, how 'bout you watch these nuts. Fuck you and that gun. They ain't stop making guns when they made yours." Houston said as my phone rang.

"Yeah." I answered the unknown number while rolling up my window on fat ass guard. If I took off running his ass would need that gun cause he damn sure couldn't chase me.

"My friend, what is taking you so long to gain clearance?" Giuseppe questioned in his Italian accent.

"Your man out here harassing us and shit G. He two seconds away from leaving with my foot in his ass." I told him.

"I will handle it." He said before the call disconnected.

"What he say?" Houston nosy ass asked.

"He said he would handle it." As soon as I said the last word blood splattered on the window where the guard once stood. "What the fuck?" I asked answering my ringing phone.

"Problem solved. Come through the gates my friend and drive to the house at the very back." He said before hanging up.

"Aye I like G. He handled that shit like a boss." Houston applauded that shit as we drove to the house I was instructed to go to. Stepped out of the car we headed up the steps where the door was held open by a butler. This nigga was too extra, butler had a fucking towel draped on his arm and everything.

"Mr. Houston and Mr. Harlem, Sir Giuseppe is expecting you. He is right this way in the dining area. Follow me." He instructed as he led the way through the house.

"Aye, why this nigga lives in a fucking museum? This shit probably cost a million dollars and its hella ugly." Houston ignorant ass called out loud as he picked up a vase.

"Alright, you know that if you break you buy applies to all ethnicities." I whispered grabbing it from him and placing it down. Catching up to the butler he led us into the dining area where G sat with his daughter at his side. I had been avoiding Kennedy's ass since we last fucked for my birthday and here she was, forced in my face. Don't get me wrong, Kennedy was one of the sexiest women I had ever laid eyes on. Her thick frame and gorgeous face would make any nigga happy. Any nigga but me. The connection just wasn't there for us and she was trying to force a relationship out of our situation When I first met G he never spoke on his family. He had just moved into the states from Florence, Italy and I was under the assumption that he was alone. We started doing business together and kept it at a business level, nothing more nothing less.

One day after leaving a meeting with G and some of his associates, I was heading to the mall so I could scoop me some shoes and Kennedy literally bumped into me. She knew who I was but I had no idea that the curvaceous beauty was the daughter of the most powerful man I knew. Her appearance screamed boss, from the clothing she rocked to the ice that was dripping all over her body. I knew she had money and the tattoos and side shaved from her head let me know she wasn't one of the boujie bitches with money, she seemed cool. We started talking and together fucked up some comas. For a month or so we just kicked it, I let her know from the jump I ain't want' nothing serious out of us and she agreed. I don't know why I believed that shit. A second after I had her thick ass sliding down my dick she was screaming how she loved me. I should have quit then but I fucked the curls out of her head that day. When she showed up at my spot the next day with groceries to cook for me, I fucked her brains out then too. The day after that when she showed up with movies and popcorn for a movie night, we ended up making a movie.

She started trying to force a relationship down my throat and I smashed the idea each and every time. The problem was I was still smashing her each and every time. Fuck the pussy was available, tight, dripping wet and was some of the best pussy I had slid in. Yeah, I would still do the movie dates with her, still let her fall through whenever I was available and didn't take the key that she had stolen from me back. In her mind, I was leading shorty on but that wasn't the case. I told her what it was and what it wasn't goin be since day one. If she wanted to keep hurting her own feelings, I would let her. Mind you I was feeling that way before I knew she was G's daughter. One day he had me pick up some information from one of his offices and her picture was all over. For a moment, I thought I was fucking the plug's young jump off but I quickly found out how wrong I was, I was fucking with the plug's daughter. She told me how the rest of the dudes she fucked with ended up dead and wanted to keep our fling on the low, so we did.

"Harlem and Houston, welcome to my home. Please, have a seat." Giuseppe greeted us standing to his feet. I felt Kennedy staring me down but kept my eyes trained on G.

"Thanks for the invite G." I nodded before finally looking at Kennedy. "Wassup Kennedy." The only reason I didn't ignore her ass is because G had finally introduced us a couple months ago. We played the role like we never met before.

"G, yo place nice but we can't ride back home with a nigga brains on the window son." Houston rude ass said.

"Houston, I always appreciate your unfiltered perspective." He said with his Italian accent. "The issue has already been handled. Niles!" he called out as the butler appeared. "We will eat." He said and Niles disappeared.

"Yo G, that's some boss shit. You got a butler and maids and shit." Houston said nodding.

"You too are a boss. Say the word and I will have a full staff at your penthouse before you make it home." He offered.

"Nah I'm good on that. I like to walk around my shit naked, dick and balls just swinging in opposite direction." His dumb ass answered. I noticed the mug on Kennedy's face. She hated Houston and he hated her. She felt like he was too immature and he felt like she could be the cause of my death.

"Well, I offered." G said as the food started pouring in. This was no regular dinner; it was a feast fit for a king. "Eat, enjoy!" he said as he took a seat and we all dug in. I was sitting next to Kennedy at G's request and it was hard not to moan out as she had unzipped my pants and had my dick palmed in her hand as she stroked it. Shorty was a pro at this shit because she was eating with one hand without missing a stroke. From previous dinners I knew that G didn't speak while eating, he enjoyed his food but Houston didn't give a fuck.

"If you want to send someone over, send your chef." He complimented as he shoved anther fork full of alfredo into his mouth. I couldn't comment on what he had going on because I was about to paint the floor with my seeds.

"Sir Giuseppe, please come with me." A maid called out as she rushed in. "It's an emergency." With those words G flew out of the room and Kennedy disappeared under the table.

Within seconds her lips were wrapped around my dick and I
was filling her cheeks up with my seeds. After licking my dick
clean and stuffing it back in my pants she sat down at the
table and finished her food.

"I'm telling yo daddy." Houston said as he fixed himself
more food. Minutes later G walked in looking worried.

"Now I need to get down to why I invited you here
Harlem." He called and immediately gained my attention.
"Because you are now family and your family is family also."
He said nodding towards Houston. I was confused and I'm
sure my face showed it. What did he mean I was family and
Houston was only family by default, we both knew him in the
same capacity? I looked at Kennedy who had a nervous smile
on her face and knew she told him about us. I would chock
her ass out later for that shit. "I see from your face that you're
shocked. Yes, I do have knowledge of you and my daughter's
growing relationship. Though I am not happy you were
sneaking around, I believe you are a perfect match for her.
Which brings me to my next point." As soon as he said that I
knew the threats would come and my throat became dry.
Picking up my glass I took a large gulp of the wine yet that
didn't seem to help. "Did you hear me?" he asked.

"I'm sorry, I zoned out. Can you repeat that?" I asked
picking up my glass again.

"My wife is very, very sick I must return to Italy but
Kennedy is much safer here. I know that you will protect her

your unborn." He said causing me to spit out my drink across the table and jump to my feet.

"Unborn? No disrespect G but I shoot my unborn down throats or on asses." I watched as his face when red and cleaned that shit up. I ain't pussy but I ain't stupid either. "Not your daughters, of course. But G, your daughter ain't pregnant by me." I said.

"My daughter was pure and untouched before you. You will step up and take responsibility for your family. Speaking of which, my daughter will not bear your child without your name." he said making me cock my head to the side.

"Daddy please, allow me and Harlem to speak. Alone." She said as he looked from me to her and then nod. Houston ignorant ass laughed on his way out the door before they were close behind he and G.

"Kennedy the fuck kind of game are you playing. Ain't no way in hell someone that was as pure and untouched as your father thinks you are was taking this dick like that." I spat.

"Harlem, I am pregnant and you are the father You are the only person I have slept with since I have moved to the states. And you will not lie and say that we use protection. Just as recent as your birthday you buried your seeds deep into my wound." She spat back causing me to laugh. "What the fuck is funny?"

"Yo ass and the fact that you're trying to trap a nigga." I said shaking my head. Truth was, she could be pregnant for me. We never used protection and *most* times she swallowed, then there were others.

"And why would I need to trap you Harlem? You can't offer me anything that I cannot provide for myself. We are having a baby and you need to deal with that. I am not asking to be with you." She lied making me side eye her ass. "I mean I did, initially. How long do you expect me to want someone that doesn't want me? I just want you to do right by me and your child." She said placing my hand on her stomach. I don't know what she wanted me to feel cause her fucking stomach was soft as shit. Kennedy wasn't one of the thick broads with a flat stomach, she had a tiny pudge but nowhere near pregnant. "My father's wife is not my mother and I hate her. I have no desire to travel to meet her nor is it safe for me. My offer is, allow me to move in with you until father returns."

"Nah you can stay yo ass right here. Offer declined." I said causing her to roll her eyes. She stepped near me and I almost slapped fire from her ass thinking she was trying to kiss my lips. Instead she brought her lips close to my ear.

"You allow me to stay with you and it will be financially beneficial for you. If my father believes we are together, then your product with be half of what you pay now. Think about it for one second. More money and in-house pussy." She whispered in my ear before sucking on my earlobe. She may have thought my dick got hard from the pussy comment but it was definitely the money that got me on rock.

Chapter 14

Houston

"Nigga, did she slip something in your drink. No disrespect G but bro ain't even the live with a female type of nigga." I laughed as Harlem really just sat here and told us that he would be moving Kennedy in with him. Like he really wanted me to believe this right now. Let me clear something up, I had no problem with Kennedy personally. I just liked to fuck with her because she was so easily bothered. If she didn't pay me any attention I guarantee you I would have stopped fucking with her a long ass time ago.

"Mind your fucking business Houston. I told you I was a grown ass man who didn't need a father I do what I want and this is what I want. No, this ain't me but it ain't about me no more. I have a child to think of." When he said it, the shit sounded rehearsed and I knew this wasn't what he wanted to do. I didn't trip because I knew he would fill me in once we left from here.

"Harlem, welcome to the family. You will take great care of my angel, I am sure." Giuseppe said making me laugh. Angel these nuts. His daughter just kissed his cheek with twin's nut fresh on her tongue. Might be a Victoria Secret

Trenae

angel but she ain't one of them flying ones in Heaven and
shit.

"I got you." Harlem assured him as he accepted the cigar
that G handed to him. I declined. Harlem told me that was
disrespectful the first time I did it but after explaining to G
that I would just waist his shit, he understood. Ain't this about
a bitch, bro came for food and left with a whole fucking
family. I let G and Harlem chop it up and took a seat back in
the living room area. A nigga was still hungry so I decided to
fill my plate up and knock some more food down. A memory
crossed my mind and I shook my head. How the fuck I go
from eating fish to laughing at the way Amanda ass spazzed
out because I didn't take her eat. I was ordering her ass room
service and she was sick of the seafood I kept ordering. Her
ass was from Louisiana so she was used to that shit and tired
of it. I loved it and couldn't get enough.

"The fuck you in here smiling about?" Harlem asked
walking in puffing on a cigar like he owned this bitch.

"Ain't nobody smiling, *dad*." I spat back.

"Aye, why you so bothered by this shit?" he asked
catching my shade.

"I ain't bothered, fuck you." I replied lying through my
teeth. A nigga was as bitter as a baby mama that just fund out
her child support was cut off.

"Nah keep that shit one hundred with me son. What's the
issue?" He asked knowing I was bullshitting.

"Look my nigga, I don't want that shit to sound like I'm not happy for you cause I am. I just feel some kind of way because you never wanted the family shit. The fine ass wife, the bad ass kids, the laid ass crib and the mean ass dog protecting my yard was all my goals. I don't feel no kind of way towards you personally, but this situation got me in my head about that. Why Leah had to fuck our shit up? This shit would have been all us by now." I told him what was really bugging me. I ain't know how to process this shit right now and what I really wanted was to face a blunt and drink my sorrows away. Kwame and Harlem thought I been falling in pussy since Amanda left but that shit ain't true. I been falling into bottles of liquor to ease this soft shit I been feeling. Like first Leah decided after all the years we invested, plans we made and love we had a nigga wasn't enough. Then I find a chick that I feel can change shit around for me and she leaves me in a fucking hotel room.

"Damn, bruh." Harlem said pulling me from my pity party.

"It's cool." I waved him off and continued eating my food.

"No, it ain't. I know how long you and Leah spoke on plans to have a family and live that life. I'm sorry that didn't happen when you wanted it to but that doesn't mean it won't happen for you soon. Leah wasn't the woman for you and Ray Charles saw that shit. She was good when you were splurging on her but when it was time to put in work her ass had a million and three problems. How the fuck she thinks you got all your money, from being under her ass?" he asked pissing me off. I still hated when people talked about Leah.

"Man, I wasn't there for her like I should have been, she wasn't all the way wrong." I defended her as usual. After the fucked up shit she did, I still felt the need to defend her.

"I'll let you believe that shit and continue making excuses for her. Check this though, I need you to chill out on Kennedy. I don't know for sure if she is carrying my child but I don't need her being stressed at all in the event that is it true." He said and all I could do is respect it.

"Bet." I responded. There really was nothing I could do but respect his mind. He was already protecting his family and I damn sure couldn't hate on that. Finishing my food, I looked at my watch.

"Aye, how long we staying here? I got some shit to handle." I lied.

"Nigga you ain't gotta lie. I gotta run it with G about some shit so you can take off." He said throwing me his keys. "Park my shit at your house and I'll come through to get it from there when I'm done here."

"Aye keep it one hundred with me really quick, what she told you to make you change your mind so quick?" I just had to know because this math wasn't adding up. When he started laughing I knew it was more to the story like I assumed.

"Nigga she made me a deal I could not refuse if I wanted to. She told me that what we are paying for our work now, would be split in half." He whispered causing me to smile from ear to ear.

"Say no fucking more." I nodded while doing some quick math in my head. "Shit nigga, tell her she can move in with me too." I laughed realizing we were about to make more money than we could count. After running it with Giuseppe, I decided to go check on My OG. Pulling up to her crib I thought back to when I brought Amanda here and had to laugh. Bella hated Amanda with a passion and I couldn't understand why. Their asses were just the same personality wise. I don't know what Bella told her but Amanda hated my moms too. I still couldn't get her blowing in Bella's face out of my head and even Harlem damn near died when I told him what happened. Stepping into the house my stomach growled like I hadn't just ate. I followed the smell of food to the kitchen and immediately lost the appetite I had.

"The fuck you doing here Leah?" I roared pissed off. Although their backs were to me I knew Leah from anywhere. I didn't give a fuck that I scared them or that Bella was shooting daggers at me with her eyes.

"Oh my God, you scared me." Leah said clutching her chest and laughing. "Hello to you too Houston, you look good." She said with a smile.

"Yeah and you look a fucking mess. I don't know who fucked you up but I hope they got one in for me. Now why the fuck are you here?" I didn't give a damn about her black eye or the bruises and cuts on her face. Leah wasn't my concern, at least that's what I kept telling myself. When I saw tears in her eyes that shit did something to me on the low, but I wasn't willing to show her that.

"So just like that you don't care about me?" She asked like this shit stemmed from nowhere.

"Ain't no just like that. You gave me your ass to kiss and now you want a nigga to give a fuck about you? WHY THE FUCK ARE YOU HERE?" I asked pounding my hand on the counter making her jump.

"Now, Houston! Lower your voice and show some respect!" Bella said making me side eye her.

"Mom, mind your business real quick. You in here entertaining her and shit like she ain't fucking the enemy. She could lead that nigga straight to your front door!" I spat.

"I would never. I needed to speak with you and I had no way to reach you. I don't have your number and I don't even know where you stay." She damn near cried out.

"Leah why would I tell you where I stay? So, you can fuck that nigga in my bed again shorty?" I asked laughing at her dumb ass. "You a snake Leah."

"That's not fair, Houston! We both played the game, you just had the upper hand! You don't think I knew about the bitches you were fucking, huh? You weren't just fucking with those bitches, they had main bitch pleasures. You were out and about with those bitches like losing me wasn't shit! I could come back from you fucking a bitch and then leaving but nooooo, Houston so many days you let the sun beat you home. Then you blamed it on trapping but you were so far above the late nights. You had niggas working for you that handled that. You made a fool of me time and time again. Krit had been trying to talk to me and I shut him down every time. Imagine my surprise when I was out shopping with Kennedy and your ass had one of these bitches with you in the mall. I didn't want to make a fool of myself so I faked like I was sick and left. That night I cooked dinner, put on the sexiest lingerie I owned and prepared to fight for my man. I ate dinner alone and pulled out my toys because you never showed.

I tracked your phone to a hotel ready to fuck you both up but I bumped into Krit in the lobby. I don't know why he was there but after not being able to get any info on your room I decided to wait in the lobby. He came over and we talked. I accepted his proposal to get a drink at the bar and one drink turned into me being lit. I poured out my heart about your infidelities and he took advantage of it. It wasn't all him though, I needed him! I needed any man that would show me that I was still beautiful and sexy. So, we got a room and that's where the affair began. Any time I couldn't reach you, I called him. I never allowed him in our home until I received a call that it was time for me to pack up. One of your side bitches called from your phone to let me know y'all had a baby on the way and you wouldn't be home that night. Minutes later you called and told me you would be working late and Wouldn't be home until the next day. That's when I began to allow him to keep your spot warm. You see we were both foul, you just had the titles, the deeds and the funds to afford it all." She said with tears falling from her eyes before turning to Bella. "Thanks for the talk. I'll go up the street and call an uber." With a kiss on Bella's cheek she ran out the door. I don't know what white movies her ass been watching if she thought I was goin run behind her.

"What you cooked?" I asked Bella as I sat at the island.

"Shit for you. You know you're as wrong as she is, right?" She asked. I could tell she was pissed off but I didn't give a fuck. I watched as she fixed herself some food and didn't get me a plate.

"Ma you really ain't goin feed me?" I asked.

"Fuck no! Go get Leah!" She spat sitting down. The baked chicken and red beans and rice smelled amazing.

"Ma she was fucking with a nigga I have beef with." I said standing and grabbing myself a plate.

"Did she know?" She asked and all I could do was shrug before she popped me behind the head. "That ain't in that girl's character and you know it! She was hurt Houston!" She said like I have a damn.

"Yeah well sleeping around wasn't in her character neither. And now I'm hurt cause the girl I love is a hoe." I shrugged before she popped me in my head again.

"Baby don't you know hell hath no fury like a woman scorned. You hurt her to her foundation and you had to deal with the monster you created. Go talk to her!" She demanded.

132

"I ain't had to deal with shit. Ma, you go talk to her! The fuck? I'm trying to eat." I said and knew I fucked up when she nodded her head and stood to her feet.

"Houston, do me a favor and stay right there!" She said heading up the stairs. I knew she was goin get her gun and that was my cue to go. Bella wasn't all the way there. Her years as a crackhead fucked her up and she would really shoot me. I still wanted some of this food so I put the plate down, grabbed all three of her pots and ran to Harlem's car. Her ass better enjoy that plate she had made cause I took her whole meal. Pulling off I rode up the street until I was on side of Leah, who was still crying. I wished there was some water around so I could splash her ass. Stopping the car, I rolled down the window.

"What Houston?" She cried.

"Get yo ugly ass in the backseat, we need to talk."

Chapter 15

Leah

Sliding in the backseat of the car I prepared myself for this conversation. I was glad he turned the music up so that I could think. It's not that I needed to think of a lie or anything, it's just that Houston still makes me so damn nervous. From the moment, we met I knew that Houston was no good for me but I just had to have him. It was the typical story, he was the bad boy that was in the streets and I was the good girl that couldn't stay away. It started with me running behind him like the love-struck teen I was. I wanted to be wherever he was although I knew my step father wasn't having it, so I lied. I would tell him I was staying over at a female friend's house when I was probably somewhere letting Houston talk me into sucking his dick. My lies were obviously working until I decided after school wasn't enough time with him and started skipping. The thing is Bella was in the streets heavy at that point and Harlem and Houston were damn near taking care of themselves, when truancy called for them they had no one to reach. The story wasn't the same for me. My step father, John, found out I had been skipping school and that started his hate for the twins.

I didn't care how much hate he had for them because it couldn't eclipse the love I had for them. Houston spoke to me about everything under the sun. We were really best friends. I knew about his past, the plans he had for the future, his hopes, his dreams and his fears. I became his diary and he became my get away from my home situation. A nigga never had a chance to break my heart because my step father had that covered early on. He and my mother got together when I was around two and got married. He legally adopted me and in my young eyes shit was good. What I didn't know is that my mom was damn near his sex slave and favorite thing to beat on. She obviously decided to no longer take it or me, so she left both of us. A few years after my mother ran off, he decided I was going to be the woman of the house. I was cooking, cleaning, ironing and against my will even fucking. That was the real reason he hated Houston, he was jealous and he had every right to be.

What he was doing to me was sick and Houston was just the nigga to end his sick fantasy. In his mind, we weren't biologically related so I should pay him for raising me, in ass. While in the house, I was not allowed to wear clothes. I was to serve him breakfast and dinner naked because he always wanted his way with me once he was fed. He told me I looked so much like my mother that being with me felt like she never left. After he came home to me wearing jeans and a tank he beat my ass. One look at the bruises and Houston told me he would handle it. I never asked what it did to him but I was never bothered by John again. I moved in with Houston and Harlem and life was good, until we moved here. I know you may have loyalty to Amanda, but Houston has always been for me. That shit ain't changing either, I'm back for my man.

"Aye get your ass out and grab one of these pots." Houston said pulling me from my thoughts. Looking up I noticed we were at a hotel and his ass had all of Bella's pots that we had just prepared dinner in.

"Did Bella let you take her pots?" I questioned knowing she didn't.

"Did you let that nigga take my pussy?" He spat back walking inside the hotel. I followed behind him without saying anything. A part of me was happy that he was being this petty about the situation, it showed that he still cared. Walking up to the desk with him my jealous side appeared when I saw how familiar he was with the front desk bitch.

"Heyyyyy Houston." She called out like she didn't see me her. Bitch was all teeth as she twirled her hair.

"Wassup ma. Let me get my usual." He told her and she handed him a key card without asking for his information. Strike two!

"What you have in those pots? It sure smells good. When I get off maybe I can come up and get a sample. I've been having these cravings." She damn near moaned while openly eyeing his dick. Strike three!

"Excuse me, I know you see me with them big ass eyes of yours. Don't let the pretty face fool you my hands are decent. And they will be all across your face honey." I spat.

"Well where were they when you were getting your ass beat honey?" She spat back. For a second I had forgot about my face being fucked up and I was embarrassed. "That's what I thought. Here you go Harlem, call me when you're done with that." She nodded my way, handed him the key and walked off.

"Bring you dumb ass on. Wanna turn red and shit cause you embarrassed. That's what the fuck You get for staking claim on a nigga that ain't for you. Better go claim that nigga Krit." He said as I followed him to the elevators. The room was amazing but I was too nervous to take it in. If I wanted my man back, it was now or never. I made my exit to the bathroom as he grabbed a plate from the kitchen and fixed his food. I said a prayer and ran water over my face before I stepped out.

"Houston?" I called out because he wasn't in sight. I noticed he was on the balcony and followed him out there. "It's beautiful out here." I said enjoying the view.

"It was until you brought yo stanking ass out here." He replied mugging me.

"Is that why you brought me here? To take cheap shots at me?" I asked forcing myself not to cry.

"Who fucked up your face?" He asked.

"Krit. He was mad because I wouldn't give him any information on you. Since the mall incident he has been going crazy with trying to end you and Harlem's life. After I refused to help him I tried to leave to come warn you and this was what that earned me." I pointed at my face as the tears fell. "And this too." I replied pulling down my maxi gown so he could see the bruises and bite marks all over my body. "He reminded me of John and I was so scared. And you weren't there for me. You said you would always be there!" I cried out unable to hold it in. Krit looked like the devil himself as he beat me over and over. I didn't expect that to win Houston over but I also didn't expect the anger.

"Don't you fucking blame that on me!" He roared slapping his plate to the ground where it shattered. When he took steps towards me I cowered against the wall and hi pointed his finger in my face. "You fucked us up Leah! There wasn't anything I wouldn't do for you. I would cut off my damn right arm for your ass! Yeah, I fucked up and fucked around and that was on me. But take some of that blame, cause you let that shit go down. I know you knew about the bitches and hoes but you let that shit rock. You led me to believe you was cool with about because of the shit you had going on. I love the shit outta you Leah but I'm a nigga with needs. Sexually you would shut down on me for months ma, months! How many times in a day could a nigga beat his own dick. I know you have issues to overcome from that fuck nigga but I had needs! I could have excused you cheating with a random nigga but my enemy? A nigga that wanted to hammer the nail in me and twin coffin. Nah that shit unforgivable." He spat before walking away. Crossing over the grass I ran behind him ready to plead my case.

"I didn't know, I didn't know about him!" I truthfully cried out. "You kept your street life in the streets! You had me out here blind! Yeah, I knew about those bitches but there was still a level of respect you had never crossed. You lost that! You started flaunting then bitches out like I'm not a woman with feelings." I cried.

"What the duck are you talking about? What type of woman says you can cheat but don't disrespect me? The disrespect is cheating! That's the thing, you never required me to respect you! When you suspected I was with a broad and not in the streets you were supposed to check that then, instead you threw ass at me. Ma, my queen will never compete with these hoes. That's where you fucked up at." He said taking a set.

"Right, so this is all on me?" I asked. "Good ole Houston did no wrong?"

"Go head on with all that Leah." He motioned for me to get out of his face but I was on some good bullshit now.

"You know why I fucked him? Huh, you wanna know why? I'm goin tell you anyway. He made me feel like I was enough. When we were together, all he saw was me. You treated me like an option and he made me a priority. When we were in our house, in our bed; he fucked me like he owned the building." I spat and when his eyes changed colors I knew I fucked up. This was the Houston that I rarely saw. The savage, my savage. Within seconds he stood up and lifted me from the floor by my neck. With both hands around my neck he slammed me into the wall.

"You like trying a nigga huh?" He asked with fire in his eyes. I could barely breath but he made my pussy jump with the way he was acting. "You wanna talk about how that nigga made you feel? How you felt when he fucked you up? Huh? When he gave you that black eye that felt good? I loved yo ass Leah, I still do. I just didn't know how to love you and I still don't. You're so broken and a nigga don't know how to fix you." He confessed with tears in his eyes. "I just don't know how to fix you." He finished releasing the hold he had on me and resting his forehead on mine. When my lips met his I knew he wouldn't reject me. This was Houston, my Houston and this was our truth. This wasn't for no one to understand but he and I. The bond we shared no one could break.

Chapter 16

Amanda

Every step I take, every move I make. Every single day, every time I pray, I'll be missing you. Thinkin' of the day, when you went away. What a life to take, what a bond to break. I'll be missing you.

Dancing and singing around the living room in just my bra and underwear, I took the bottle of Cîroc to the head hoping it eased the pain and stopped these tears that seemed endless. I needed that numb feeling to overtake the pain I was experiencing. I just didn't want to feel it anymore. I wanted to feel anything but this emptiness I felt. This has been my reality for the past week. Seeing Mannie's mother put me in a horrible place. Her manly ass looked just like him and seeing her reminded me of all that hurt I attempted to suppress. Finally. being able to tell her everything I wanted to say since she banned me from his funeral was somewhat of a relief, not much though. I was never able to say my final goodbye to the only man that loved me more than he loved himself. I'll never forget our last moments together.

"Damn Panda, all of this for me?" Mannie smiled when I woke him up with breakfast in bed after blessing him with some bomb head.

"I could ask you the same, all of this for me?" I replied waving around the house Mannie worked overtime to make a home with me. I

wasn't just grateful for this home, I was grateful everything Mannie exposed me to. He real life introduced me to real.

"You know you my lil mama, I got you through whatever. Why you tearing up? What's on your mind?" he asked.

"Mannie, I am so grateful for everything you have done for me." I said wiping my tears. My emotions were getting the best of me in that moments.

"Ma, I told you stop all that crying. This right here is faith." He said. Mannie told me how he wasn't supposed to be in McDonald's the day we met. The female he was dealing with, Kim, begged him to get her some cookies so he stopped. As we ate all of those damn meals he ordered, he filled me in on their situation. It was going nowhere fast and she refused to let go. They weren't a couple but you couldn't tell that to Kim and Pam. His mom loved her and she was convenient so she stayed around. After he met me they were still dealing with each other because he and I were just friends. As soon as I was of age, he ended their fling and it was Mannie and Manda since. From that point on he said faith made him stop at that McDonald's and not the five that he passed up. "I told you stop thanking me, I'm doing what your man is supposed to do."

"No Mannie, let me finish please? You gave me hope when I thought it was all lost. I wanted to give up on life and then God blessed me with you. He saw that I was standing on my last leg and then their you were to carry me. You were a breath of fresh air in this grimy polluted world. When you first saw me, I was a dirty teen looking for a cheap burger. I was used to the nasty attitudes and dirty looks but from day one, you saved me from that shit. You made sure there wasn't a person alive that could look down on me I'll never forget trying to get my clothes from the

laundry mat and you made me throw them away. It was so hard because that was all I had left in this world and you were asking me to leave it behind." I said taking a break as the memory made me break down. Abandoning his breakfast Mannie pulled me onto his lap and gently rocked me.

"Ma, you good." He said in that sexy raspy tone. He wasn't asking if I was good, he was telling me. That was another thing he did. Mannie never asked if I was good. He told me he knew I would always be good and he would make sure of that so there was no need to ask what he already knew. Pulling myself together I continued to speak from my heart.

"It was so hard Mannie, but you asked me to trust you and I did. In that laundry mat, I threw away everything but the clothes on my back. The crazy thing is I never felt like I was losing everything, I felt like I was finally gaining everything. You proved that feeling right. Mannie, you gave me life, when death was looming near. I never told you but in that trash can I left behind the two bottles of Tylenol PM I stole from Family Dollar. That night, I planned on heading to the park and taking both bottles. I'm not exaggerating when I say, I owe you my life. I will forever love you and only you Emmanuel." I finished before collapsing in his arms and soaking his shirt with my tears. I felt his body stiffen beneath me.

"Ma, you fucking with me right now, right?" he questioned. "How was you just goin take my soul mate from me like that? I don't care what life gives you, you better push the fuck forward. If I don't open my eyes tomorrow, you better push the fuck forward. You don't owe me shit because everything I gave you came with no strings attached. This house,

that's paid for and in your name shawty. You held me down like a nigga couldn't imagine. I had some niggas that left when shit got tough but you went to war with the kid. If I lost something you got it back. I never wanted you to see the street side of shit but when I had my back against the wall, you covered me. When I first saw you, I never saw a dirty teen." He lied making me cut my eyes at him.

"Mannie, stop lying." I laughed through the tears.

"Nah man, check it. I saw you in the laundry mat that was up the street. I was at the red light when you went through the trash and grabbed the old bottles of laundry detergent. Real talk, I sat there and watched you fill them with the water from the washing machine, shake it up and pour it on your clothes. I pulled off and made a stop then hit up McDonald's. There you were just trying to eat and that bitch was giving you a hard time. I didn't see you as a dirty teen, I saw a survivor. I didn't know your situation initially, but once you told me what was good I was in awe. Most females in your position would sell pussy or just fold but that wasn't you. I planned on feeding you, throwing you some cash and dipping. That changed when I spoke with you. I saw the pain in your eyes but you held a conversation like your situation was regular. So how could you play it like that but want to end your life?" he asked.

"It was regular to me. But regular doesn't make it easy. That day you fed me my stomach was touching my back. The was my first time eating in two days. Nothing is regular about that." I said before my voice broke. *"How could I not want to end my life? Living was so hard so death had to be easier."*

"Nah this ain't you talking, ma. You my soldier, you don't quit. I told you this was faith. You have too much to offer the world and it

would have been selfish to deprive us of your beauty and talent. I'm happy as fuck that I met you on that day. When I count my blessings, I count you twice. You don't give a fuck about the clothes, cars, money, the ice or my reputation. You see Emmanuel when everyone else hype off of Mannie. I can't buy that type of feeling. I can't reward that type of love. If I don't give you anything else, I give you my word that I got you for life and even after that. Even when my casket drops, you will live like the boss lady you are." He said placing a kiss on my forehead, kissing the tears falling down my cheeks then finally finding my lips. I got lost in the moment and didn't even notice he pulled his dick out until he eased me down on it.

Mannie and I fucked all over that house until I fell asleep satisfied and exhausted. I don't know how long I was asleep but when I woke up the sun was long gone, I was in bed alone and someone was banging on our door. There were only three people who knew where we lived. One was Loc, Mannie's right-hand man, Pam and the other was Ashleigh. No one showed up without calling first so I threw a robe on and grabbed one of Mannie's guns.

"Mannie, are you here?" I called out to the empty house. It wasn't anything new to wake up in bed alone. Mannie was in the streets and I know that late nights came with the territory. I knew my man wasn't doing me wrong because there were numerous times I hit the block with him. If I called, he answered. I was wifey to a hustler, I knew how this went, or so I thought. No one prepared me for what was to come.

BANG BANG

Trenae

"Who the fuck banging on my door like the motherfucking police?" I spat.

"Amanda, this Loc. Open the door ma." His tone of voice should have told me something was up. He was so serious. Loc was never serious prior to that. I had never seen him without a smile on his face until I opened that door.

"Mannie ain't here Loc." I said opening the door with the gun at my side. "He supposed to be with you. If you're here who watching his back?" I questioned.

"Aye, sit down for me real quick." He said making my body go stiff. All kinds of thoughts ran through my head.

"Please don't tell me my man is in jail." I said assuming that could be the worst-case scenario. When Loc walked over to the couch I sat next to him. There was an awkward silence before I spoke again. "Umm, you going to tell me where my nigga at or nah?" I questioned again.

"Look, I need you to let me speak without cutting me off. I got some shit to tell you and its important you remember it. After that I'll tell you why I'm here. Behind your favorite thing in the house, is a safe. The code is all zeros followed by how many kids you and Mannie want to have together. In the drawer with your panties, there is an area that you can pop out and there is bank information, you're the only person that can access that." He said causing me to nod my head and stand to my feet.

"Ok, let me just get dressed and then we can get the money to bond him out. I know his ass has the cash in the safe." Without waiting for a response, I bolted out of the living room. After taking a hoe bath, I threw on a maxi dress and some sandals before heading back to the front. I asked Loc to wait for me in the car before I went to my favorite thing in

148

the house. The picture I took of Mannie. I looked along the side of it and for the first time noticed a little button. After clicking the button, the picture opened. Mannie was going to have to explain this shit to me when we got home. When he got this shit done? Entering the code, 004, I laughed. Mannie told me I was crazy because I wanted four kids until I told him why. In the event that Mannie and I died, I never wanted my kids to be alone like I was. At least they had their siblings to lean on unlike me. My eyes bulged once the safe was open. There was a folder and a few guns in the safe but the amount of cash that was in this safe is what shocked me. I knew Mannie was getting money but I never asked how much money. Grabbing a few stacks and throwing it in my book sack purse I placed everything back like it was then headed to the car where Loc was waiting.

"You good?" I asked him once I got in. He looked as if he was stressing and I didn't know why. "They didn't catch him with anything on him, right?" I asked getting pissed. "I been told Mannie stupid ass to stop riding dirty. He got those hoes to do that shit for him." I had put Mannie onto the idea of paying some of these thots to let him store drugs in their house. Their houses were in the area that he would sell in. He didn't turn their houses into a trap, because he never sold there. It was just easier and safer to grab work from their house and head up the street over riding around town with it. I was so caught up in my thoughts I didn't notice that Loc never answered me. I didn't even notice where we were until he called my name.

"Listen Amanda..." he started.

"Why are we here?" I asked noticing we were at Lafayette General. "You playing, but I need to go get my man out of jail so I can fuck him up." I said.

"Man listen! I been trying to tell you but Mannie ain't in jail." He screamed with tears in his eyes. Suddenly it clicked.

"Was he shot?" I asked shaking my head.

"Yeah." Loc answered before crying hard.

"Why are you crying? Just pray. Mannie is a fighter, no matter the condition he will shake back." I said with too much faith in my man.

"Sis, he died about an hour ago. He never made it by me. Somewhere between your house and mine, he was killed." He cried out causing my heart to drop. The pain I felt was released in the form of a scream. This couldn't be true. Not Mannie, not my Mannie. He promised me forever and a day and I was cashing in on that promise. My body violently shook as I cried enough tears to flood a river.

"Nah, this ain't true. Mannie would never leave me." I said in denial. Unbuckling my seatbelt, I ran through the hospital. I didn't know where to go or who to look for but I was on a mission. Turning the corner, I heard Pam before I saw her. Her wails were ringing in my ear and hearing her scream not my baby made it all real for me. In that moment I knew, I had lost my lifeline. Loc appeared on side of me as I shook my head at the news.

"Sis..." Was all he was able to get out as I collapsed in his arms.

"Loc, he told me we were forever. He promised me that he had me through anything. How he just going leave me alone? Loc, I need him to survive." I cried out. "HE TOLD ME WE WERE FOREVER!" I screamed into his chest. What felt like moments later I was waking up

with an IV in my forearm. Looking to my right I saw Pam on the phone.

"She's up." She said before ending that call.

"Pam, what's going on? Can I see Mannie?" I asked her. She never really liked me so to see her here was shocking.

"You fainted." She answered without looking at me. "You know I told Mannie you weren't shit. I told him Kim was the woman for him. They've been together since middle school, you know. That's how I knew you weren't shit, you walked your ass right on in and fucked up their relationship. Well look at your karma, he's gone. And I guess it's back to the streets for you, gutter rat. You almost did something right, but then your weak pussy couldn't even hold the baby." She spat as Kim opened the door like she was invited.

"Pam let's go. we have to make arrangements for Mannie. My baby needs to go out in style, like a true boss." She said pissing me off. The machines went off as I attempted to sit up.

"Bitch Mannie ain't your baby." I spat.

"Well now, he's neither of ours." She said blowing a kiss my way just as the nurse came in.

"I'm going to need you to step out for a minute while I calm her down. I'll come get you when she's stable." She told Pam.

"No need to. The only part of her that I wanted to be bothered with, died with its father. Oh, and Amanda, don't you bring yo ass to that funeral. Kim will not be disrespected." She spat before storming out with Kim behind her. Looking at the nurse she answered my unasked question.

"Yes, you were six weeks pregnant but you had a miscarriage." She confirmed causing me to cry out. Why did God hate me so much? Thanks to an infection, I was in the hospital for a week and couldn't go to the funeral if Pam would have allowed. Mannie was buried and Pam wouldn't tell Loc or I where. I went from graveyard to graveyard all over Lafayette, searching for him. I had even tried to follow her to see if she would go visit him. That only lead to her calling the police on me. I slipped into a depression that I couldn't shake until Mannie spoke to me from the grave. Once the bills started piling up I finally opened the safe. Sitting in a Manilla folder on top of some documents was a letter from Mannie to me.

"Panda, I know if you're reading this God wrote The End to the fairytale you've had me living in. Damn ma, I wanted forever with yo fine ass but he had other plans. You think I saved you but Amanda you saved me. I was beasting through these streets with no purpose before you. I wasn't even moving smart because I feared nothing. Meeting you put fear in my heart. I feared the thought of losing you. There ain't a woman alive or dead that can take your place ma. You the one girl. You that one in a million as female niggas spend their life searching for. Thank you for finding me. Thank you for loving me. Thank you for holding me down. It breaks my heart to know that you have to read this letter and I'm not there to stop the hurt. That shit hurts more than whatever took

me out, I can guarantee you that. Do me a favor ma, wipe your tears. This money, I was putting up to get out of the game. You wanted the big family and although you said you would live in the projects with a nigga, you were too good for that. I was going to buy you the house, the cars and the clothes that Oprah would be jealous of. After that I was going to fill you up with my seeds, fuck four we were going have a football team of kids. I guess life happened. Do me another favor, with this money do everything I wanted to do for you and more. Take Ashleigh on a trip and go see the world ma. When you done with that settle down with a man, not a real nigga. Find you a man that will make a fool of himself to see you smile and give that man some kids, while he gives you the world. You will know when it's real when you have to question it. Go with it if the question keeps you up at night Panda. Don't let my death turn your heart black ma, please. Do that for me. It's going be people that ain't goin want you to be happy, boss up on them Amanda. Shine like I would have told you too. Panda, you're my best friend and the best thing that happened to a nigga. No matter what the world brings your way remember a nigga love you as deep as the ocean, and a lil bit deeper than that. Take care baby.

Trenae

What a life to take, what a bond to break. I'll forever be missing Mannie.

Chapter 17

Harlem

"Babe, we are starving." Kennedy said walking in front of the television screen. It was Sunday morning and as usual I was laid back playing Madden. The difference was, I was in the living room instead of in my man cave, which was really only an extra bedroom that I filled with game systems and a big ass television. It had only been a month since Kennedy has been living with me and I had to give up that room. She kicked me and my game system out of the bedroom and was setting it up for the baby. At first, I wasn't so sure if she was having my baby but I warmed up to the idea of fatherhood the moment I heard the heartbeat. I took her to Bella and she confirmed that Kennedy was carrying my baby.

"Kennedy bruh, you know Sunday is the only time I have to chill so that's what I'm fixing to do, chill! We just went grocery shopping and we have a shit load of stuff in the kitchen." I said grabbing her waist and moving her from in front of the television.

"Harlem, I don't want anything in the kitchen. I want to get out of the house today." She whined stomping her feet like a child. I cut my eyes at her and continued playing my game. When she stomped away I already knew her extra ass was about to show out so I waited for it.

Kennedy staying here hasn't been as bad as I thought it would have. She isn't blowing up my phone when I'm gone and when I come home there is always a hot meal waiting. All I have to do is hit her line when I'm on the way in to see if she is craving anything and I'm good to go. Kennedy been treating me like a king, bath water waiting on me and I even had to stop her ass from washing my nuts and drying me off. Her ass been watching too much Coming to America. I know the reason she hasn't been pushing a relationship in my face is because we damn near in one. She doesn't have to do those retarded ass pop ups on my ass because she lives here now. If I would have known shit would have been this easy I would let her slide through and stay a while ago. The thing is I know this is business and I don't think she does. The only thing that has changed is our sex life. Kennedy is always offering the pussy to me on a silver platter and I've been constantly denying her ass. I don't want her feelings to get involved more than they are because as soon as those prices get reduced and her pops is back in town, she just my baby mama. That shit sound harsh but it's the truth. A baby wouldn't give us a title that I refused to give before she found out she was pregnant. I liked Kennedy because she was cool. It was no secret that I was attracted to her because baby girl was bad as fuck. The problem is, that was all she was. She relied on her pops money and didn't want anything but to be the wife of a nigga with power and money. There was nothing to make me fall in love with, she was fine as hell but lacked depth.

Thinking of Kennedy's flaw made my mind drift back to Brooklyn. Over a month has passed and I couldn't forget the stranger that had captivated my mind in five brief days. I wanted to say fuck her and move on but then another part of me wanted to sweep all of Louisiana, find her and drag her ass back here. I found myself comparing the two to each other often. It's like I'm trying to force myself to see a future with Kennedy, and thoughts of Brooklyn is blocking that shit. Kennedy is made to be the wife of street nigga, she understands this life. See when shit goes left in the streets, me turning into a savage doesn't scare her. That shit doesn't move her one bit. She grew up around killers and drug lords so my status doesn't impress her. The glitz and glam makes everything worth it for her and there lies my problem. If shit goes left and a nigga is looking at football numbers, shorty is on to the next baller.

Kennedy the type of woman to show up looking good and smelling better to every visitation. I know that from the conversations we had. I know that fuck boy was treating her bad and she was still loyal to him. I wanted to call shorty dumb for waiting on a nigga potential but I quickly realized that, that was her loyalty in question. When he was making money, she was there and she felt like it would be fraud of her to leave him. I did drop in her ear that if that was the only problem then I could respect that but don't let loyalty make you that nigga dummy. I thought I got through to her but I guess not. Our conversations were effortless and deep. She knew how to keep my mind and my dick stimulated at the same damn time. I didn't have to worry about if she would stay down if the money dried up because she proved that daily at home. I knew she wasn't used to the finer things when I took her shopping. She checked price tags and wanted to kill me for spending tons of money on her. When I handed her my card, she brought just what she needed for that night. Lil mama had a black card and didn't get anything extra.

"This has been fun." Kennedy spat dragging her suitcase in front of the television. I told ya'll she was going to cause a scene. I couldn't help but to laugh as I shook my head.

"Kennedy where you going?" I asked placing the controller down.

"Why do you need to know? You don't care about me or my baby. You do not care if we starve. All you care about is your little game. I'm so sick of this Harlem! Why don't you love us?" She asked crying her heart out. This shit was so funny to me. Every single time her ass got hungry, I had to deal with hangry emotional ass Kennedy.

"Kennedy, yo ass ain't starving. I made you breakfast and it's just about to hit noon. You ate your food and mine shawty." I laughed.

"You see you don't take me serious. Why are you laughing at me Harlem? You know I am eating for two so I don't appreciate you counting my plates." She said still crying. Standing to my feet I walked over and removed the suite case from her hand. That shit was light as the fuck and she know her ass needed movers for all the shit she had here. Her ass just wanted my attention and for some reason she got it.

"Come here ma." I said grabbing her hand and leading her to the couch. I sat on the couch with her straddling my lap and really watched her ass cry over food. "Ma, quit crying. You know I hate that shit and I don't want you stressing with my seed." I said wiping her tears away then gripping her thighs. "I'm going feed your ass." I laughed when the smile on her face spread from ear to ear.

"Oh my Gosh thank you soooo much Papi." She moaned out while doing a lil happy dance in my lap. I wanted to ask her what kind of fat shit that was but there were two things stopping me. One, her ass would start crying cause I said fat. Two was, the way she was dancing in my lap had me on brick. I could see from the lust in her eyes she noticed it too. "Let me handle that for you." She moaned out.

"Nah, yo ass starving remember. We about to go find us something to eat. Where you think you going in this short ass skirt though?" I asked slapping her thigh.

"The same place you are going with those grey sweatpants." She replied back.

"Fuck what you talking about, all these niggas ain't about to have a peep show to my baby mama's goods. Go change! "I said.

"Fuck what you talking about, all these bitches ain't about to have a peep show to my baby daddy's goods. You go change." She spat my words right back at me. Nodding my head, I respected her gangsta and we both went change then shot out to a lil spot in Harlem named, Amy Ruth. She was crying about their brunch so that was the move. Pulling up I thought I saw Harlem's jeep so I hit his line only for it to go unanswered. That seemed to be the normal lately. We met up when it was time to work but I hadn't really been hanging with him outside of that because of Kennedy. She didn't force me to do anything but on the cool she's been occupying that void that I was feeling since meeting and losing Brooklyn. Was it completely gone? Hell no, she just made that shit a lot less noticeable. I figure he was still out entertaining these broads so I let him rock. I noticed Kwame was missing in action too, they was grown so I wasn't questioning shit.

"See, isn't this nice?" Kennedy asked as we finished up our food. All I could do was nod because my mouth was full and she was right. The food here was bomb and the atmosphere was chill. I wouldn't mind bringing Kennedy around here when she wanted to. "Harlem..." She started but paused and started biting her lip. I knew she did that when she was nervous.

"Speak your mind?" I asked swallowing my last piece of chicken.

"I was thinking..." she paused again.

"Shawty if you don't let me know what's good, we are going have a problem." I told her sitting up and checking my surroundings.

"Dang, let me get it out. "She nervously laughed and rolled her eyes. "Things have been good with us. We don't argue unless I'm hungry, the house is always clean, you always have a hot meal and I treat you well. On top of that we are about to welcome and baby into the world together." She started.

"Yeah." I replied waiting for the rest.

"Well, I'm not baby mama material Harlem. I want more." She said starring in my eyes. I noticed the water already chilling the corner of her eyes and didn't have time for the drama she would bring.

"Let's talk about this home." I lied knowing I wouldn't talk about shit once we left here.

"No." she said grabbing my arm and stopping me from standing up. "You will just drop me home and we will never talk. Harlem, I am an attractive woman. I know you are attracted to me even if you try to deny your feelings. I know what we have isn't love but there is something there. In the middle of the night, when you are asleep and I get out of the bed to use the restroom you reach out for me. I've watched you feel around the bed and then your eyes pop open when you don't feel me near you. You stay awake until I climb back in the bed, pull me near and then you finally fall back asleep. You want to have sex with me and I know you do but you stop yourself. Why is that?" She questioned searching my eyes for some truth.

"I don't want your feelings to get too invested..." I started before she cut me off.

"You mean you don't want your feelings too invested. Harlem, I love you. It's too late to stop my feelings and you know that. You knew that when you agreed to my proposal of me moving in. You allowed me to move in not for the money, but because you're feeling me. Tell the truth." She pleaded.

"What I feel for you isn't love." I said giving her the truth that she wanted to hear.

"I didn't say it was. But there are feelings, right?" she probed.

"Yeah, some." I nodded.

"I can work with that. Harlem, if you allow me I can be what you need. We are already starting a family. Don't allow our child to be born into a broken home."

"Who said our home is broken ma? My child will have everything it desires. There is nothing I won't do for my seed." I replied.

"Except keep its mother happy?" she said letting the tears fall.

"Keeping you happy is what I've been doing. My child's health depends on your happiness." My statement must have been the wrong thing to say because she stormed off to the bathroom crying. Throwing money on the table I followed her into the women's restroom. She was crying so hard her body shook. I grabbed her and wrapped my arms around her.

"Why won't you love me Harlem?" she cried.

"Ma, I think I'm in love with someone else." I finally admitted. Her body got stiff and the tears stopped.

"Where is she then? If you are in love with someone else how are you always with me? Where is she?" she asked sounding as if she couldn't breathe.

"I don't know. It wasn't that serious to her." I said shrugging. Suddenly a smile spread across her face.

"So, I still have a chance? I still have a chance at winning you over?" she asked.

"I'm not saying that."

"Harlem, if you do not see this woman again then those feelings die. Just give me a chance to make you happy? Please?" she begged. What did I have to lose in this situation? She was going to be around regardless and Brooklyn was long gone somewhere miserable with her nigga.

"Alright, Kennedy." I replied. She jumped up and down before placing a kiss on my lips.

"I promise you won't regret this. Now go, I need the restroom." She said before kissing me again and running into the stall. Walking out of the restroom I bumped into a woman walking in. "My bad ma." I said looking in my phone.

"Harlem?" A familiar voice called out.

"What's up Leah?" I said pulling her in for a hug. Leah was like a sister before she played my brother like a piano.

"Mothing much, about to head to the mall." She replied. She looked a lot better than the last times I had seen her. Not that she looked rough, it just wasn't her. Standing in front of me was the Leah that I knew when she was dating Houston.

"That's what's up, take car ma." I replied walking away.

"Ok, tell your brother I'll be right out." She said making me turn around.

"Huh? You're with Houston?" I asked.

"Well duh. Who else would I be with? He didn't tell you we were back together?" she asked.

Chapter 18

Ashleigh

I was sick of trying to reach Amanda and getting her voicemail. I knew she was going through things, but so was I. A week after the incident at my house, I went through with my plans and got the eviction notice done and Dre was served. After going to court, they gave him thirty days to leave. He had seven more days before it was time to go and he was still there. That's how long it had been since I talked to my best friend, over a month. The thing is, when she went into her missing Mannie spells, she refused to allow me to be around her. Normally these only lasted a week so this was different. I feel horrible for not being there for her like I should but I was going through it myself. I lost my job because all four of my tires were flattened and I missed one day. I was all out of vacation time so I had a limit of three days to miss. The next two days were missed consecutively when I got sick. I could barely crawl out of the bed except to vomit. Well my job didn't give a fuck so they let me go. Bills still needed to be paid so I did what everyone else was doing but with a twist. I opened an online boutique and offered online styling services. They paid for the clothing and we would video chat on how to dress for their shape and budget. Business was booming and I was happy about that.

Dre spent a lot less time drunk but that didn't make it better. Sober Dre was deadly to my wellbeing. During the day, he was out looking for work and at night he was begging me for forgiveness. Like now, he sat here on his knees telling me how he hadn't touched a bottle since the day he did that horrible shit to me. I heard him crying out at night as he tried to beat his addiction to alcohol but it was too late. I didn't want anything to do with Dre and he needed to realize that.

"Ashleigh, can't you see that I am trying? I've been looking for jobs day in and day out. I have an interview next week." He said with a smile like that would change anything. My head felt heavy and my mouth was dry so I reached for my water but he beat me to it and held the bottle to my lips. I took a sip of water before he removed it from my lips and closed the bottle. "You don't look too good. Let me put you in the bed?" he offered.

"Deandre, you need to be packing instead of worrying about me, I'll be just fine."

"Ashleigh, I fucked up. I know that and I feel horrible for how I treated you, let me make it up. We been together too long for you to just end that like this." He continued pleading.

"Dre, you ended it. I accepted too much shit from you over the years and I'm finally tired. I deserve to be happy." I responded.

"And I can't make you happy?" he asked. I didn't even respond. I simply laughed and shook my head. "I made you happy for years before shit went left."

"Yeah you did, but we can't live in the past, now can we? That bottle got in the way of the man I loved." I replied.

"Exactly, so my present is the man you see right here. The bottle is gone, is the desire still there? Hell yeah, but I now know that what we have is more important than that. The man in front of you knows that this is what's worth fighting for." He said motioning between him and I. "Ashleigh, you told me that what we had was forever. When we first met, I was there for you through all the problems you had. I loved you past your hurt and you can't love me past mine?" he questioned.

"There isn't hurt for me to love you through Dre. You just like to drink, nothing more nothing less." I grabbed my laptop and stood to my feet. I didn't realize how dizzy I was until I fell into Dre's arms.

"You good?" He asked me placing me back on the couch.

"Yeah, I think I just moved way too fast." I said shaking my head. The room was still spinning so I didn't attempt to stand again.

"You don't look Ash. Let me take you to the hospital?" He offered. I wanted to object but the way I was feeling had me a little scared. I knew diabetes ran in my family and I remembered my grandmother used to have these dizzy spells, so I needed to get it checked out.

"Grab my purse off my bed and let's go." I said giving in.
***

"No, I can't be pregnant." I cried as Dre sat there smiling like he won the lottery. The whole time we had been here he sat texting on his phone and I couldn't understand why I was bothered by that. I was done with him. The thing was I very much could be pregnant and we both knew that. What he didn't know was that it was a possibility the baby wasn't his. The doctor let me know that I couldn't be any more than 5 weeks pregnant but I would have to find out for sure with my gynecologist. The dates would add up for around the time that I was with Harlem and when Dre took advantage of me. I think that's what hurt the most, this could be Dre's baby. Dre was the type of person to take this inch and run with that shit. He would use this baby to ruin my life. Moments later there was a knock on the door and it swung open. I expected a doctor but was shocked to see Shirley, Dre's mom.

"Hey son." She greeted Dre before turning to me with a smile. "Ashleigh." Was all she said before pulling me into a hug. The whole scene shocked me because I was under the impression she hated my guts.

"Ms. Shirley, it's nice seeing you but what are you doing here?" I asked.

"Deandre texted me and I think it's time we had a talk, woman to woman." She said looking at Dre who knew it was his cue to leave the room. He walked over and kissed my forehead before making his exit.

"Umm, I'm not sure what we need to talk about." I truthfully told her as soon as the door closed. This woman had one conversation with me when Dre and I first started dating and nothing afterwards. I ran through possible conversation points in my head and came up blank. We definitely had nothing to talk about, in my opinion.

"I see so much of me in you that it is scary." She started. "And Dre, he reminds me of Andre, his father. And that too scares me. You need to know that Dre filled me in on some of the things you two are going through but I know there are always three sides to each story; yours, his and the truth." When she paused I jumped right on in.

"No disrespect, but what reason are you here today? I thought you hated me. You told Dre to stop dating me and when he wouldn't you stopped talking to him. How could you hate me so much that you stopped talking to your own son?" I asked.

"I don't hate you Ashleigh, I pity you. I see that pissed you off but let me explain why I say that. I knew you and Dre would travel down this road before you hopped in the car. I didn't want that for you. When we sat in my kitchen and spoke the very first time I met you, I know you were too good for what my son would put you through. I knew you did not deserve the pain he was going to bring to your life. You had everything figured out. You had goals and you were so focused and driven. That smile on your face when you spoke about your future plans lit up my house. As soon as you left, I told Dre to leave you alone because you were not the girl for him." She said pissing me off.

"But how could you say that when there was nothing wrong with me? If I had a son, I would want him to date a woman like me."

"And if I had a son worthy of you, then I would want him to date a woman like you also. You see Ashleigh, you aren't the problem now and you weren't the problem then. Dre is his father's child through and through. Andre used to get so drunk, then beat me until he was sober. I couldn't do anything right in his eyes. If the wind blew too hard on Thursday morning, it was my fault and he beat me for it. If he got home and I cooked corn when he felt like I should have cooked baked beans, I woke up with a black eye. Dre was around for every beating and every sip his father took. He started telling my baby, liquor cured everything and women needed to get beat to behave." She shocked me with that revelation. Mr. Andre' was the perfect man the few times I had met him. They seemed so happy together.

"I haven't even seen him lift a beer bottle before." I said still shocked. "I've seen him around you, he treats you like you are China. That man watches every move you make like he's worried that you will break if you fall and he isn't around."

"Baby, you see our present situation not our past. When Dre was 13 his father decided to start him drinking when I would be at work. I had no idea that was going on. It wasn't until I came home from work, early one day that I learned of that shit" she paused wiping the tears that came to her eyes. I could see the memory still pissed her off.

"You don't have to tell me anymore." I told her as she got herself together.

"No, I need you to know. I came home from work and Dre was asleep. Now that was weird to me because Dre was always waiting up for me when I got home. I didn't bother him though, I went to the kitchen to fix myself dinner. I always cooked before work and they would just warm up their food when they were ready. I noticed the food was untouched that day. It wasn't unusual for Andre to drink and go to sleep without eating. He would wake up sick and then put something on his stomach. I was concerned with my baby though. I woke Dre up to see if he had anything to eat and when he yawned I smelled the liquor on his breath. I immediately noticed he was drunk when he was fully awake. When I asked him why did he drink his father's liquor he shocked me by going into the closet and getting his own stash. Andre had purchased him his own fucking stash of liquor. That night, I took my baby and never looked back." She paused and wiped her eyes once again. A nurse walked in and checked my vitals before stepping out again, leaving us alone.

"It was three years later when Andre lost his brother to Cancer. He was in a bad place and drinking heavier than ever." She started again. "I went the funeral because I was once very close with his brother and that was the first time he laid his eyes on me since I left him. I thought I would hate his guts but I didn't. I still loved him, I just loved my son more. When he fell on his knees at his brother's coffin, I was there helping him up. We talked, I told him that he made my son an alcoholic. It was so hard on me because I couldn't send my son to rehab, they would investigate me. I stayed home to make sure my son kicked the habit and was successful at it. Andre asked me to help him and I did. It's a process for me every day so I already know it's the same for you. I know my son has been taking you through hell and back again. I'm not here to convince you to stay with him nor am I here to tell you to leave him. My son asked me to come and tell you his story and that is what I did." My heart began to hurt for Dre. How could a child go through so much at the hands of his own father?

"I'm so confused." I confessed.

"I know you are dear, so was I. My husband makes me so happy every single moment of the day. He would fight God if he put a frown on my face. He made a promise years ago that he would make my days so beautiful it would be had to remember the past. I'm not there yet, as you saw earlier, but I don't regret going back to him. Every story won't be like ours though. Decide on if you can love Deandre as he attempts to be a better man. It, however, is not your obligation to do so. If you feel like this is too much and can live without Dre, then you know what to do." She stood to her feet and kissed my forehead. "I will tell Dre he can come back up. My husband is taking me out for dinner. Take care of my grandchild." She said leaving me alone with my thoughts.

Chapter 19

Amanda

Flipping the covers off of my head, I decided that I was over moping around this house like a damn zombie. My hair, nails and feet were a mess and my skin had lost its glow due to lack of sunlight. My home was a mess and I'm sure I picked up some weight from all the take out I had been eating. I know I needed to get it together and quick. I hadn't spoken to Ashleigh in over two months and that was all on me. In the midst of crying, I threw my phone at the wall and it shattered. I ordered a new one and it got delivered over a month ago but I didn't bother setting it up. Climbing out of the bed I fell to my knees and did something I haven't done in a long time, pray.

"Jesus, I know you haven't heard from me in a while but I really need you. I'm trying down here really, I am but nothing is working. Lately I haven't been able to figure out whether I'm coming or going and I'm sick of it. My heart hurts so bad and I know that only you can fix it. Make sure Mannie is comfortable up there for me please? Allow him to come soothe this hurt I'm feeling, even if momentarily. Mannie baby, I just need a sign. just one simple sign to let me know that you still have me through whatever. I can't wither away in this bed anymore. Help me make it through this day and the ones to follow. Amen." Climbing off of my knees I began stripping the sheets from my bed and went to the laundry room to load them with the dirty towels I neglected.

It took me three hours to get my house the way it was before my meltdown and I was able to shower. After washing my ass and my hair I felt like a new woman. Going into my closet, I slid on an olive-green romper and paired it with a pair of camel and gold sandals. My hair was still wet and I was going straight to a salon so I allowed it to naturally curl up. The thick gold hoops were the only accessory I had on besides my camel colored cross body purse. A little lip gloss and I was out the door. Hopping in my Audi, I sped to ElleQue's Beauty Bar to let my girl LaQuinta hook up my hair like only she could. God was on my side because her chair was empty and she could immediately take me. I had little patience and would complain if I had to wait so, look at God! Relaxing in her chair, I decided it was way too hot for my bundles.

"You dead ass wrong for having this hair like this Amanda. What are we doing to this bird's nest? You know I have some new 360 frontals in, right?" She asked freeing my hair from the bun I had threw it in.

"No, it's too hot for all of that. Shit be having my hair all stank and sweaty. Can you hook me up with those braids everyone wearing?" I asked pulling up my phone and showing her a picture of T. I's wife, Tiny rocking some tribal braids.

They were nice and I was in love with them. I even wanted the beads she had at the end.

"Yep I got you. But the dude who owns the barber shop across the street about to bring me some food. Is it cool with you if I eat real quick, I promise it'll take 15 minutes for me to finish." She assured me.

"Yeah do your thing, I have to program my phone anyway." I replied as she started blow drying my hair out.

"So, where you been?" Laquinta was cool and all but she knows I didn't like anyone in my business. I was cool but I was far from friendly.

"Here and there. You know me, I never sit still." I gave her a vague answer before I pushed my face into the new iPhone 7 plus and began setting it up. I heard the door open but still didn't look up. From the smell that blessed my nose, I was sure it was ole dude with her food.

"I'll be back." She said walking off. The aroma was calling my name so I had to ask.

"Where that food came from?" I asked knowing I was going get a plate as soon as I left here. The smell was begging me to leave now and get a plate.

"Reggie's soul food. A new lil spot that opened a week or so ago." A deep voice answered causing me to finally look up from the task of personalizing my phone. I was greeted with a smile that was very familiar. "Damn you can ask about food but ain't got love for an old friend?" He asked.

"Oh my God, Loc!" I squealed abandoning my phone and purse and jumping in his arms. "Where have you been?" I asked. For months after Mannie's death we kicked it tough. It's like we were each other's calm in the storm. Loc made sure I was straight and I did the same for him. Out of nowhere he crushed me when he told me he had to shake the spot, whatever the fuck that meant. I felt like I was losing a best friend and in a crazy way I did. Loc had quickly became my confidante. Once he left we stayed in touch for a while and then life happened. I found a passion for traveling and he was somewhere doing him. I didn't even know he was back here yet alone that he was a barber.

"I went to Atlanta for a minute to clear my head. Lafayette was suffocating me." He replied running his hands through his hair that was wildly flying around. "I was tired of the streets, shit wasn't the same. Niggas ain't made like Ma... like they used to be." He looked awkward and I already knew why.

"I'm past that level of grieving. You can mention Mannie's name." I assured him. I know he was worried, there was a time I would throw a fit anytime he mentioned Mannie. I'm better now.

"That's what's up." He nodded in approval. "I was worried about you ma. I'm glad you doing good. You still look like the wife of a boss." He complimented me causing me to blush. I used to have a little crush on him even though I knew nothing could come from us. I think it had something to do with him being somewhat of a hero to me. He really saved me from myself back in the day. "Anyway, after leaving the streets I went to school. Got my license and now I own two barber shops." He smiled and I was genuinely happy for him.

"Good for you Loc! You look happy about that and I'm proud of you." I said just as Laquinta called me over.

"Aye, put my number in your phone. And use that shit, we need to catch up." Nodding my head, I handed him the phone before he left to go handle his clients.

"Soooooo, you and Loc?" Laquinta asked.

"Soooo you and these braids." I replied back. After an hour, I walked out the shop a new person. Something about a woman doing her hair will do that to ya. I wanted to go straight to the nail salon but decided I would treat Ashleigh. Pulling up at her house I peeped the brand-new Tahoe and wondered what company she had. I rang the doorbell and she swung it open mugging me.

"What?" She spat.

"Poo, I'm sorry. I was going through it in the worse way and I'm sorry. I never should have closed you out but you know how I get. I can't control my emotions sometime." I explained hoping she wouldn't give me too hard of a time. "Anyway, I wanted to treat you to the nail bar." I grinned before she threw her nails in my face then pointed at her toes.

"I wanted to treat you for once and you didn't answer your phone or your door when I came by." She said finally allowing me in the house. I noticed she had new furniture, a bigger television and all her decorations were upgraded.

"What you done hit the lotto?" I asked noticing something different about her. "You don't look the same. What changed?" I asked.

"I didn't hit the lotto but Dre came into some money. Oh, and nothing has changed with me. Except I'm carrying a baby. And you weren't here to celebrate with me!" She started crying. All I could do was stare. What the fuck just happened? I thought to myself. Just as I began patting her back the door swung open and Dre came in.

"Baby are you ok?" He asked rushing to her side. This was the most attentive I had ever seen him and the shit spooked me.

"I'm fine my love." She answered wiping away the tears.

"You sure? Can I get you anything? Are you comfortable?" He fired off questions without waiting for an answer.

"I'm good Dre. Let me talk to Amanda." She told him and he actually got up and walked away like an obedient child. This was definitely the wrong house or something.

"What's going on?" I asked as soon as he was gone.

"Nothing, we are working on being a family." She replied with a forced smile.

"How far along are you?" I asked for my own reasons. The look in her face let me know that she knew my reason.

"Don't do that Amanda. We are in a good place so don't fucking do that." She whispered.

"Harlem needs to know." I whispered back.

"Ok sure. Do you have a way to contact him?" She asked making me shake my head. Before I left I deleted my number from Houston's phone and I had never programmed his.

"We can fly back there." I suggested.

"No, we will leave it the way it is. I am finally getting the family I want!" She said with finality in her voice. I didn't argue back because something told me she would regret this decision.

Chapter 20

2 years later
Ashleigh

"Hey Dre, how are y'all doing?" I asked stepping outside so I could hear him over the noise.

"We good over here, stop worrying about us and enjoy your evening. It's your last night as a single woman." He answered reminding me that we were less than 24 hours away from our wedding. Although I was well aware of that fact, I couldn't explain why my heart suddenly felt like it would burst from my chest. I always thought when I would think of my wedding day I would feel that warm giddy feeling, not a full out panic. Truth is, I pushed this wedding off for as long as I could. I always found something wrong with a venue the closer it got to the wedding day and it bought me another few months to find another. When Dre proposed two years ago he told me he didn't want a long ass engagement, maybe four months tops. I gave him the exact opposite of what he was asking. We would have still been procrastinating had he not have me a short time limit about 2 months ago and an ultimatum. Dre said if we weren't married by his birthday, we were going to the courthouse to say I do. For a woman who always dreamed of the big wedding, this was a deal breaker for me. I couldn't not marry Dre, he was a very crucial part of my family. I even went out of my way and invited my mother because it was important to me that she saw that although she wasn't in my life, I had a family anyway.

"Okay Dre, I'll be home no later than 10 o'clock. See you then." I said.

"See you at the altar. I love you." He called out.

"Me too." I answered before ending the call. Spinning on my heels, I headed back inside of the party to find Amanda. I have no idea why we decided to come to all-star weekend for my bachelorette party but here we were and I don't regret it. We weren't even here for the game, just the parties. Like now, we were fucking it up at P. Diddy's all white party. I won't say we were the baddest females here but I will say I didn't see anyone fucking with us. Amanda was turning heads in a white body con dress that had her whole right side of her hip and thigh cut out. She went for a more basic look while I upped the ante. The wide leg jumpsuit I had on was sheer with white stripes and it exposed the white bra and white pair of panties I wore underneath. My hair was in its natural state and my face was beat thanks to Amanda! Like I said we may not have been the baddest in here, I just hadn't laid my eyes on fucking with us just yet.

"Wassup sexy." I heard as my arm was grabbed. Spinning around I was eye to eye with a coulda been. He coulda been something special had it not been for the neck up. I was well aware how the men of today's time didn't take well with rejection so I simply flashed my ring. "Damn." He mumbled eyeing it. I flashed a smile and walked away. Anytime someone saw my ring they had that reaction. I was aware that it was bigger than average and I told Dre he went overboard. When he came into some money a couple years ago, he really upgraded us. We had a bigger house, new cars and he started his own company. I was proud of him. Dre had not touched alcohol in two years and was an amazing father so that made life a lot easier.

"Hey, I was just coming find you. Everything okay?" Amanda asked over the music.

"Yep, just checking in." I said grabbing the shit she was offering. Just then they played our song and we started fucking it up. If your woman heard, "Cash Money Records taking over for the 99 and the 2000" and she didn't drop whatever she was doing and fuck it up, leave her! It was my last night as a single woman and I was making the most of it. Bending over at the waist, I grabbed my ankles and shook my ass as if rent was due and I was a stripper. Amanda silly ass started making it rain on me and that just called attention to us. Coming up and placing my hands on my knees I started twerking like I had done so many times in the comfort of my own home. I was never a big dancer in the club but you couldn't tell that tonight.

"Ayeeeee that's my bitch, fuck it up!" Amanda cheered me on as well as the people in our surrounding area. I notice a stank look one of the females was giving me so I made sure I spun my ass in her direction as I squat low to the ground and made each ass cheek jump to the beat. Once we got to the drop it like it's hot part it was a wrap for me. My feet hurt and I didn't have to drop it like it was hot, I was really hot.

"I'm too damn old for this." I laughed with Amanda as she rotated her hips and ass to the sounds of R. Kelly seems like you're ready. When a stranger came over and jumped in sync right behind her I couldn't take my eyes off of them. He placed a hand on her exposed hip and the moved as one, that shit was sexy. They demanded attention and got it. The movements were so sensual I wanted to hand his ass a condom. As soon as the song ended, my bitch walked off like a model, leaving him stunned and pitching a tent. I followed her lead and we made our exit.

"Chile, I had to get out of there, that man almost made me fuck him silly in a room full of people." She laughed as we made our way back to the hotel room. The hotel wasn't far from the venue but thanks to the heels we rocked, we still caught a cab.

"You had that man drooling though." I laughed as we exchanged a high-five."

"What about you though? You were fucking it up tonight with all of that." She hyped me as she slapped my ass. Walking in the room we both kicked off our shoes and threw on some slides.

"Hell, you only have one bachelorette party, right?" I asked shrugging.

"That's what they say. Speaking of which, who has a bachelorette party with only two people in attendance, including their selves?" Amanda asked making me roll my eyes.

"People who don't fuck with new bitches." I responded sliding the key card onto the table and removing me jewelry, except my ring of course.

"My fucking feet are killing me." She whined as I looked in my suitcase for my night clothes. I had already decided, I was going to enjoy the remainder of my night from bed. "I'm going get ice." She called out leaving out of the room. After finding what I was looking for, I looked up and noticed Amanda ass left the door open like we weren't in New Orleans. I loved the city but these niggas out here were a different kind of savage and played no games. It was nothing for them to walk in your shit like you invited them in. I went to close the door but was obviously too late. Before I could shut it so that it would lock it was being forced back open.

Chapter 21

Harlem

"Damn ma, I thought you would be happy to see a nigga. Instead after all this time you slamming doors in my face and shit." I told a shocked Brooklyn. I thought I was tripping when I saw her ass earlier but I guess that wasn't the case.

"Ha- Harlem?" She asked with shock evident in her face. I watched as she opened and closed her mouth as she looked for the words to say and I refused to help her ass out. Although I was positive it was her when I laid eyes on her earlier, being in her presence has my head fucked up. It didn't help that time had treated her well. Besides the fact that she had a lil more ass and hips and a lot more breast, she looked the same. Her hair was in its natural state and the fact that she was wearing the fuck out of this outfit had my dick hurting in these jeans. The jumpsuit was sheer so I had a full view of all she had to offer. I hungrily took her in with my eyes because I knew any second now I would wake up from this dream that began earlier today.

earlier

"Harlem, how do I look?" Kennedy asked spinning in a circle. I watched the way her fat ass jiggled in the skin right white dress and my dick reacted.

"Like you trying to get something started." I told her pressing my dick against her ass so she could feel how hard she had me. My shit was on brick and she needed to handle that.

"Harlem, no. I want to get out of this room." She stomped her feet like a child. I was used to this so it didn't faze me one bit. Her ass would never grow out of that.

"And I'm trying to fuck, sooooo..." I left that sentence as it was because I was already lifting her dress over her ass and ripping her thong off.

"Harlem, I said no!!! My hair and makeup is already done and you said we could go to the party tonight." She whined making my dick deflate. I was so pissed off that she was once again telling me no. She hadn't given me any ass in months and I was tired of settling for her basic head. I didn't even want to be here, she knew all these people in one area didn't sit too well with me. Who the hell told her foreign ass about All-star weekend anyway? Now she was in my ear crying to go to P-Diddy's all white party and I just wasn't feeling that shit.

"Yeah man fuck. Go see if Vontavia, Toya and Leah ready to roll out with you and we just goin meet y'all there." I told her flopping back in the bed. I watched as her face frowned up.

"First of all, don't you ever insult me like that Harlem! Why do you keep trying to make Leah and I hang with a bitch that was fucking our men?" She spat.

"Aye, watch who the fuck you talking to with all that fucking attitude. I ain't trying to hear that shit. It's been two fucking years since Kwame and Vontavia made that shit official. Over two years since the bitch was close enough to look at my dick yet along suck or fuck it. You worried about her more than Kwame is." I told her tired of having this conversation.

"Harlem how would you like it if I invited you to party with one of my exes?" She questioned with her hand on her hips.

"Difference between you and I is your ass lonely, I got my twin and my cousin. Believe it or not, Vontavia nor Toya fuck with you like that either. They fuck with you off the strength of me so you would wanna watch your mouth. They don't give a fuck about who you are, they were raised in the streets. They will fuck your ass up and then I gotta hear your mouth about it."

"Fuck you!" She spat before fixing herself back up and walking out of the room. Kennedy was going to forever be Kennedy. Over two years together and I still wasn't in love with her. I had love for her and had grown comfortable with her but that was about it. Being with Kennedy was out of convenience. A year and a half ago, Giuseppe's wife ended up beating cancer and he decided to spend time with her. Luck wasn't on his side because they were both murdered while they slept in their home months later. That put Kennedy in a position she happily passed on to me. With some requirements, of course. Houston, Kwame and I became the niggas you needed to see if you were trying to make moves. I thought we were bosses before but the shit we were on now was some next level shit.

There were murmurs in the streets that niggas were at our heads but no one was making any noise. I had a loyal team that was down for us and in return them niggas was eating so much you would think they had a tapeworm. Life was beautiful for us. Kennedy was cool but I needed more. She would never be that woman of substance I was looking for and though she was fine with that I wasn't. I tried talking her into opening a business or some shit like that but her ass wasn't biting. She had access to money that her children's children would live off of and had no problem telling me so. My phone ringing made me jump up and snatch it.

"Yeah." I answered Houston's call.

"Get yo ass up, wash ya nuts and let's go. Nigga if you saw the stampede of ass I just saw then you would beat me out that room. These bitches down here thicker than Bella grits." His dumb ass slurred through the phone. I already knew Houston had been drinking and was about to show his ass tonight.

"Nigga why you worried about ass, didn't you bring Leah?" I reminded him.

"Leah know we ain't together. Her ass just don't know I booked a second room because I'm goin have fun tonight.

She said we were friends so that's what it is. But aye I'm coming that way in 15." He said ending the call. I couldn't help but to shake my head at him and Leah's relationship or friendship as they called it. Leah had been trying to prove she was a changed person for two years and she still hadn't noticed that he just didn't care. I think his ass gave up on love while she was still trying. I heard banging on the door and knew it was Kwame's ass so I swung it open.

"The fuck you banging on my door for?" I asked mugging him then shaking up with him.

"To get your ass out this room. Who the fuck comes way to New Orleans and just watches tv?" He asked inviting himself in.

"A nigga who didn't want to be here anyway. Let me find out Tavia over there dressing yo ass." I nodded towards his fit. That shit was nice it just wasn't him.

"She went cop this when she saw me trying to wear black." He said laughing. Only this nigga would try to roll in an exclusive ass party wearing opposite of what they required. "You know black is my color. But get yo ass dressed." I didn't respond, I just grabbed my shit and started getting dressed.

I had already showered and shit with Kennedy so It didn't take me anytime. Rocking a pair of white Balmain jeans with the matching button down and a pair of white Balenciaga sneaks a nigga looked like money. I through a diamond stud in my ear and a gold Cuban link chain and bracket to complete my look. I was still wearing my hair faded on the

sides and Kennedy had threw some braids in the top potion
so I was ready to go. A couple squirts of some Paco Rabanne
one million cologne and we were out the door to scoop up
Houston. This nigga was lit and Kwame was right with him
turning up as we mobbed our way to the elevator. Just as it
was closing a nigga mind started fucking with him. I could
have sworn I saw Brooklyn in the elevator rocking the shit
out of a white jumpsuit.

"The fuck wrong with you?" Houston asked me as I stared
at the closed doors. I was trying to convince myself not to run
down those stairs and meet the elevator on the next floor.

"I thought I saw someone." was all I said. Accepting the
fact that I just wanted to see her so I did and not that it was
actually her. When Kennedy asked to come here, I damn near
prayed that this was the part of Louisiana she stayed in. After
listening to a bunch of the locals talk I realized their accent
was different. We went to the party and cut the fuck up. I
wasn't normally the party type but this shit was live and the
drinks had me feeling good. I decided to dip out early and
head back to the room. Wanting a drink, I realized our ice had
melted and went to get more. I walked out of our room
heading to the ice machine and this thick female walked out
of her room in front of me. Lil mama was bad as fuck but she
was walking with a purpose only to stop at the ice machine.
When I caught a glimpse of her face and heard her talking shit
on the phone I made a U-turn back to the room she just came
out of. If Amanda was here then I'm positive that was

Brooklyn I seen earlier. Walking to the door it was slightly open before I heard her mumbling.

"Bitch goin leave that door open like we not in New Orleans." I almost dropped the ice bucket because if I didn't know anything else, I knew that was her fucking voice! Before I could knock the door was closing so I pushed my way in. And now here we were, just starring at one another.

Chapter 22

Ashleigh

"Ashleigh, I'm sure somewhere in America it is frowned upon to cry over your fling while you're at your wedding." Amanda said as she attem*pted to do my makeup once more.*

"You didn't see how hurt he was when he left. You didn't see how broken he was when he saw this ring and I had to tell him that I was engaged. Then he refuses to take any of my calls!" I attempted to stop myself from crying out again. I was all kinds of fucked up because she was right. I was a couple of hours away from saying I do and I was crying over Harlem and what was supposed to be a weeklong fling we had. I couldn't help it that my heart cried for him. Memories of the previous night flooded my head.

    ****

"Ha- Harlem? Oh my God, how are you here? How did you find me?" Shocked was an understatement. I never thought I would see him again yet her he was causing my heart to skip quite a few beats. Even though years had passed the feelings were the same. Harlem was the comfort I had been missing. I have no idea how to put it in words but basically, he gave me a vibe I couldn't find anywhere else. I loved Dre and I was so proud of the strides he made as a man, but a part of me felt like it was too late. I was constantly trying to fall back in love with him but it just wasn't working. I think my problem was staring me in the face.

"Damn. I had so much to say to you and now that I'm in your presence and nigga lost for words." He said letting his eyes roam the length of my body. He looked so fucking good in his all white attire and I wanted to ask how did we miss each other at the party but I zeroed in on those lips. If my memory was correct, those lips held the power to put me under a spell I never wanted to shake. I saw them moving but couldn't tell you nor did I care what they were saying. Not able to resist him any longer I jumped in his arms and our lips met as I wrapped my legs around him. He fell back against the door under my weight but that didn't stop him from gripping my ass. Those lips were everything I remembered and more. I felt his dick pressing against my pussy and knew that the night turned around for the better. When he started fumbling with the zipper on my jumpsuit I caught my head.

"Wait, Amanda is rooming with me." I said.

"I'll handle that, go take that shit off." He told me pulling out his phone. Before I walked in the bathroom I heard. "Aye I got a package you been waiting on, come handle that. This package been missing for two years." He laughed before hanging up and I closed the bathroom door. After all the dancing, I did at the party I knew I needed to take care of my girl so I started the shower and stripped from my jumpsuit and underwear. I hoped in and lathered up quickly because I could hear Amanda's mouth just outside the door. Without knocking her ass burst in the bathroom.

"I'm happy about your lil reunion or whatever but where the fuck I'm going sleep while y'all fucking?" Her ghetto ass asked. "Oh, and I accidentally told him your real name. You been playing with that joke for too long." She said laughing. I would never forget that name I told him, after all I named my daughter Brooklyn.

"Aye Ashleigh you covered up?" Harlem asked.

"Ugh yeah." I answered not knowing why he was asking that. Seconds later Houston strolled in the bathroom like he owned the mother fucker. He hit me with a head nod then picked Amanda up off her feet. Ignoring her scream, he tossed her over his shoulder and walked out, closing the door behind him. Did he just kidnap my friend? Knowing she was in good hands I got out of the shower, dried off and applied lotion. There was no time for playing so I walked out ass naked and wasn't the only one. Harlem's body had definitely improved over the years. He been fine but now that man had the body of a God. The tattoos that graced his body had even grown in number. I must have taken too long admiring the work of art because he approached me with his dick stiffly leading the way.

"Ma, we can make love later but this ain't that right now." He warned before lifting me up like I was nothing. I simply nodded right before he shoved his dick in my wet pussy. His lips found mine as he rotated his hips to allow me time to adjust to his size. I let him know I was ready by bouncing my ass up and down his dick as my juices slide down to his balls. Pushing my back against the wall he started the punishment that was two years overdue. Harlem began drilling into me like he was digging for gold. The slight right curve of his dick made my mouth fall open but my words were caught in my throat. This nigga was fucking me silent. When he hit my spot, yeah that spot, my voice was back with a vengeance.

"Oh, my Gooooodddd. Harlem! Fuck me baby! Fuck me please!" I begged because my life did depend on this nut that was begging to erupt. Harlem was the only man that had the key to my flood gates and I was ready for him to use it.

"You know how much you fucked me up Ashleigh? Just leaving me like that?" He roared as he took out his anger on my pussy. I know that I was supposed to be getting punished but this shit was just what the doctor ordered.

"Oooohhhh, I swear I'm sooo sorry. I'm so sorry!" I moaned matching his thrust as I rode his dick. Tightening my pussy muscles, I felt him grow harder signaling that he was ready to nut. "Cum with me baby." I moaned in his ear as that feeling built up in the center of my body. The warmth traveled down to my legs and the flood gates opened as he erupted with a loud groan. He placed me on my feet and if this was still my Harlem, he wasn't even close to being done. "The ass got fatter, you sure you can handle it like this?" I asked bending forward and grabbing my ankles. He didn't even answer with words, he just forced his dick back into my slightly swollen pussy and I welcomed him home once more. After a few rounds of earth shattering sex we laid in the bed in silence.

"I still love you." He blurted out after about fifteen minutes of silence. "The shit won't go away." He confessed.

"I will always love you, and I don't want it to go away." I followed with a confession of my own. "If life was different you would be mine and I would be yours. I wouldn't have to go through another couple of years without you. In fact, I don't know how I'll walk away from you a second time. The first time was nearly my death." I spoke my truth.

"You don't have to walk away a second time. You didn't have to walk away a first time but the past is the past." He said grabbing my hand in his. I decided to change the subject.

"Harlem, who is Harlee?" I had to ask because when I saw the tattoo on his neck this jealousy formed that damn near brought me to my knees. I felt his body go stiff and knew she meant something to me. Selfishly I was pissed. "It's ok, I don't even want to know." I told him with a shrug.

"Harlee was my greatest love and greatest heartbreak all wrapped into one." He said with so much emotion it devastated me. "She was my daughter. But she was never able to live the lavish life I had planned for her. After 9 beautiful months of preparation she never made it. She was still born." Without looking up I knew he was crying. I felt the tears in my hair. "I didn't know I wanted a child until I heard her heartbeat. Then she was all I thought about only for it to be snatched from me." He said. Looking up I kissed away his tears and laid my head back on his chest. At that moment he didn't need words, he needed me to just be there. I couldn't speak anyway, guilt was eating me alive.

"I'm sorry." Was all I offered. There was a little more silence before he broke it.

"I see you have some new art too." He laughed and I know he was referring to the tattoo that said Brooklyn and Harlem. "Let me find out you love a nigga so much you got the name tatted on you." He joked.

"I do though." I laughed.

"So, what's stopping us from being together?" He asked the question I wanted to avoid.

"Harlem, are you still with Harlee's mom?" The way he stiffened told me what his mouth didn't.

"Something like that." Was his response.

"No need to lie, I'm unavailable too." As I said that his finger ran over the massive rock that weighed my finger down. It wasn't his first time running his finger on it but this time was different. He knew the meaning. Looking in his eyes I saw the hurt that filled them and immediately wanted to take it away.

"You're..." he paused to clear his threat. "You're getting married?" He forced out. A single tear slid down my face as I nodded my head.

"When?" He asked and looking at the clock on the wall I realized it was my wedding day and I was in the bed with someone other than my fiancé.

"A few hours." I whispered. "We leave at 8 and my wedding is at 5." His grip on my hand tightened.

"It's cool, at least I had tonight. You want me to go or..." he asked leaving the ball in my court. I didn't answer him verbally, instead I went under the covers and slid his dick into my mouth. If this was the last I got to enjoy him, fuck sleep. With tears in my eyes I rode his dick for the remainder of the night before collapsing onto his chest. We wore both sexually and mentally drained so sleep came easy. When the sun rose, so did I. It felt like a slap to the face when I woke up to an empty bed. Harlem left a note that I refused to read. I knew he poured his heart out in that letter and begged me to be with him but I couldn't. I belonged to another man and in hours we would be a family.

****

"If you don't stop all this crying while I'm doing your makeup." Amanda popped me pulling me back to reality. "If you want to leave then we can bounce. I got a full tank of gas and I'm parked up front. Shit I was hoping yo ass changed your mind." She said dead ass serious. "I didn't even wear heels in case we had to run for it." She pulled her bridesmaid dress up and was wearing a pair of chucks. Her ass was nuts.

"How can I do that to Dre?" I asked.

"Fuck Dre! If at any time you want to leave we can. He don't scare me plus I'm strapped." Going into her clutch she pulled out a gun.

"He's changed so much for me Amanda. The kids love him and he loves them. I'm sorry but I can't." I said as there was a knock on the door. Amanda went to open the door *then returned with a smirk*.

"If I can't talk you out of this shit I know someone who can." She smiled as Harlem turned the corner in a black suit.

Chapter 23

Harlem

"Noooo Harlem you can't be here. You've already made it so hard for me to go through with this." Ashleigh stood to her feet as tears started flowing. "Please leave, you can't be here!" She begged. Leaving wasn't an option. I don't know why I came here, but the moment I saw her I knew I wanted to be the most selfish man alive.

"Can you give us a moment?" I asked Amanda.

"If y'all need a getaway driver, let me know. I filled up and in parked out front." She whispered in my ear before leaving.

"Man, you look beautiful." I told Ashleigh as I looked her over. The dress was made for her. In fact, it would just be a plain old dress on anyone else. On her, it was breath taking. "Does he know you were supposed to be for me? Does he know how fortunate he is to stand in my place on what was supposed to be my wedding day?" I had to ask her the question that was tugging at my heart. Ashleigh most certainly was made for me.

"Harlem please don't make this harder than it has to be?" She pleaded with me.

"That's not why I'm here ma. That's not why I'm here at all. I never want you to feel the way I felt when you walked out on me years ago. When I left out of your room this morning, I thought it was to protect my heart. I knew I wouldn't be able to allow you to walk out of my life twice in one lifetime, so I walked out of yours. But if that hurt you even a fraction of how it hurt me, I needed to protect you from that. I didn't want to be the reason you were devastated on your wedding day, so here I am."

"Don't you know that seeing you here knowing you're not who I'm meeting at the altar hurts me more? I wish you were mine Harlem. I wanted all of you, sweet Harlem, and even the savage Harlem that the streets get. I spent plenty of nights wishing you were my savage. But faith wasn't on our side. And I'm ok with that. You will be an amazing husband one day."

"I wish it was today, ma. I didn't come here to hurt you. Dry your eyes and enjoy your day. I wish you the best." I said kissing her lips.

"How did you know where I would be?" She questioned through tears once we parted.

"Your girl Amanda really hates your nigga. She made sure I knew where this would take place at. But I'm not here to ruin your day. A nigga really wants to see you happy, even if it is with a fuck boy." I laughed and she slapped my chest.

"I love you Harlem, forever." She declared.

"I love you too. Brooklyn." I laughed as I thought about how my first memory of her ass was a lie. Kissing her forehead, I left the room while I still could.

"You got your woman?" Houston and Kwame both asked me.

"She's not mine, let's go." I told them heading for the doors.

"Nah bruh, the wedding about to start." Houston said grabbing my arm.

"You think I want to see her marry someone else?" I mugged him.

"Look, Amanda said if shit didn't work out between y'all in that room that you needed to see something at this wedding. And since I'm driving, we goin see something at this wedding." He said as he and Kwame walked in the opposite direction of the exit. I followed their lead as they sat at a table filled with older women and we waited for the wedding to start. There weren't many people in attendance, maybe like 100, so I had a clear view of the aisle. Everyone was so happy and that shit was passing me off because I was sitting in my seat dying. Just as I was pulling out my phone to call a cab, an uber or something, the doors opened and music began playing. Her fuck boy walked out smiling like he won the lottery. Actually, thinking of that, she told me she was footing all the bills when we first met. Looking at how everything was so extravagant, I wondered if shit turned around for him or if she was footing this bill too. Her ring wasn't some lil cheap ass ring either. I watched as he walked up and shook the pastor's hand before the doors opened again. This time Amanda walked out. I laughed aloud because her ass refused to smile, instead she looked our way then nodded to the door. I didn't understand the gesture until the doors opened again. My breath got caught in my throat and I was well aware of the fact that Houston and Kwame were staring in my face.

"Oh my God, look at Brooklyn and Harlem." One of the women cooed as the children walked down the aisle.

"What you just called them?" Houston asked.

"Their names, Brooklyn and Harlem." She answered trying to focus back on the kids. I couldn't take my eyes off of them. No man, she wouldn't do that to me. I told myself over and over. Especially not after I told her I had lost a child and how much that hurt. She would have told me.

"Who kids?" He asked her again.

"Well the bride and groom of course." She answered rolling her eyes.

"Nigga, those children look just like us. You know like I know his bitch ass ain't had no parts in the makings of them." He told me before turning to her. "They about what, going on two?" He asked her.

"You sure want to know a lot about their children. They are twins and they made two a few days ago. I'm trying to watch the wedding could you be quiet." When he frowned up his face I knew she fucked up. This nigga already couldn't stand old people.

"You worried about a wedding when your old ass needs to make sure your funeral planned. Fucking fossil." He spat and if I wasn't so focused on the fact that Ashleigh was making her way out I would laugh. As if she felt my eyes on her she stared dead at me and I notice her eyes flicker to the front where the kids were stand and then back to me. Tears filled her eyes and I knew in that moment she was guilty. Damn, she really never told a nigga about his seeds. I watched as she sat on side of that nigga and exchanged vows with my children between them like one big happy family. As soon as I heard her ass say I do, shit went left.

"No, the fuck you don't. I know the fuck you don't with my seeds standing right there." I said loudly standing to my feet as all eyes turned to me. Ashleigh began shaking her head no but fuck her, I was on some good bullshit now.

To Be Continued...

CPSIA information can be obtained
at www.ICGtesting.com
Printed in the USA
LVOW07s1819110817
544663LV00011BA/677/P